Sherlock Holmes:
The Hunt For Moriarty

A play by Nick Lane

Based on the work of
Sir Arthur Conan Doyle

First edition published in 2025

Paperback ISBN 978-1-80424-099-1
ePub ISBN 978-1-80424-100-4
PDF ISBN 978-1-80424-101-1

Published by MX Publishing
335 Princess Park Manor, Royal Drive, London, N11 3GX
www.mxpublishing.co.uk

Cover Designed by Adrian McDougall
Featuring Ben Owora, Mark Knightley, Pippa Caddick, Gavin Molloy, Robbie Capaldi and Eliot Giuralarocca
Photography by Alex Harvey-Brown

BLACKEYED THEATRE

Resident at South Hill Park in Bracknell, Blackeyed Theatre is one of the UK's leading mid-scale touring theatre companies, and since 2004 it has been creating exciting opportunities for artists and audiences by producing theatre that's audacious, accessible and memorable. Blackeyed Theatre has two principal objectives through the work it produces; to provide audiences and artists with fresh, challenging work; and to make that work sustainable by reaching as wide and diverse an audience as possible. Over the past few years, Blackeyed Theatre has balanced these artistic and business objectives by creating new, exciting versions of established classics in unique ways and by identifying relevance with today's audiences.

Recent new commissions include *Dracula*, *The Great Gatsby*, *Sherlock Holmes: The Sign Of Four*, *Jane Eyre*, *The Strange Case of Dr Jekyll & Mr Hyde*, *Frankenstein* and *Sherlock Holmes: The Valley of Fear*.

Blackeyed Theatre strives to make its work sustainable by producing theatre that audiences want to see in ways that challenge their expectations, by bringing together artists with a genuine passion for the work they produce, and through an appreciation that titles of work with a wide appeal can still be performed in ways that push artistic boundaries.

blackeyedtheatre.co.uk

Sherlock Holmes: The Hunt for Moriarty

This play was commissioned and first produced by Blackeyed Theatre in 2025 in association with South Hill Park Arts Centre and Theatre Royal Winchester. The production opened on 4 September 2025 with the following cast:

Dr. John Watson	**Ben Owora**
Sherlock Holmes	**Mark Knightley**
Mrs. Hudson Violet Westbury Irene Adler Hilda Trelawney-Hope	**Pippa Caddick**
Inspector Lestrade Louis LaRotière Professor Moriarty Alex Trelawney-Hope Herbert Fennell	**Gavin Molloy**
Sir James deWilde Rail Officer Hugo Oberstein Ronald Smith Don Chappell	**Robbie Capaldi**
Mycroft Holmes Col. Valentine Walter Wilhelm von Ormstein Henry Petty-Fitzmaurice Will Parfitt	**Eliot Giuralarocca**

Artistic Team

Writer and Director	Nick Lane
Composer/sound designer	Tristan Parkes
Fight director/choreographer	Rob Myles
Set designer	Victoria Spearing
Costume designer	Madeleine Edis
Lighting designer	Oliver Welsh
Projection Designer	Mark Hooper
Company Stage Manager	Jay Hirst
Assistant Stage Manager	Duncan Bruce
Producer	Adrian McDougall

Foreword

This adaptation began, as many things do, with a foolish idea shared by me and Adrian McDougall, Blackeyed's Artistic Director: "What if we followed up the productions of *The Sign of Four* and *The Valley of Fear* by taking several of Conan Doyle's Sherlock Holmes stories and stitching them together with an original plot? And, just to make it spicier and more enticing, what if we centre it around Holmes' nemesis, Professor Moriarty?"

A modest proposal, really. A bit like deciding to reupholster the Sistine Chapel because you've got a new colour scheme in mind.

A year of writing, rewriting, plotting and working-out later, here we are, a play that interweaves a selection of Conan

Doyle's short stories; *The Adventure of the Bruce-Partington Plans*, *A Scandal in Bohemia*, *The Adventure of the Second Stain* and *The Final Problem*. And while I've done my best to remain faithful to Doyle's world - foggy streets, clipped dialogue, and a detective who makes the rest of us feel like we have the intellectual capacity of a labrador - I've also nudged the timeline forward to the year 1900. Why? Because the turn of the century, the Second Boer War, and the twilight of Queen Victoria's reign offered a backdrop too rich to ignore. History, after all, is the best kind of supporting character: always present, rarely upstaging.

More importantly, I wanted to explore something Doyle himself often did — using Holmes' fabulous adventures not just to solve crimes, but to probe the anxieties of his time. In that spirit, this play tries, to some degree, to reflect on a number of our own contemporary concerns. I won't spoil what those are — you'll spot them, I hope, between the deductions and the disguises.

So, whether you're here for the mystery, the monologues, or the mild existential dread, I hope you enjoy the ride. And if you don't, well...

Blame Moriarty.

Nick Lane

Act One. *The stage is the char-blackened ruin of a once great and familiar location – the study at 221B Baker Street. All of the furniture has a similarly burned look, and as well as the music playing as the audience enter, we also hear the destructive lick and crackle of flame. At FOH clearance, the opening music begins, and slowly, across the space, carrying a variety of burned boxes, files, books and other items, come members of the Metropolitan Fire Brigade. This is a choreographed piece of movement and at a particular point in the music, WATSON enters. He stands in the space and looks around slowly. Replacing the sounds of fire come echoey lines of dialogue:*

HOLMES	*(Off; rec'd)* I fear we've rather upset the hornets' nest...
MORIARTY	*(Off; rec'd)* Once you dam up the flow of truth...
HOLMES	*(Off; rec'd)* Oh, you are clever, Professor...
MORIARTY	*(Off; rec'd)* ...you can hold back words like 'good' and 'right' until they're useful...
HOLMES	*(Off; rec'd)* Watson, your memoirs will draw to an end...
MORIARTY	*(Off; rec'd)* Join me... your intellect, my vision...
HOLMES	*(Off; rec'd)* ...the day I crown my career with his capture...

MORIARTY　　　　　*(Off; rec'd)* ...we'd be unstoppable...

HOLMES　　　　　*(Off; rec'd)* Or his extinction...

WATSON shuts his eyes these last two lines echo and fade as MRS. HUDSON enters upstage. She is reading a letter. The last of the MFB exits. Music fades. Lights.

MRS. HUDSON　　　Well. That's it then.

She hands the letter back to WATSON. A beat.

There's no way he might... *(have survived the fall)*

WATSON shakes his head.

No. No.

Looking at the devastation around him, WATSON moves downstage as if to a window.

It's not as bad as they're saying. Brickwork, lick of paint...

WATSON gives a slight shrug.

I was out at the theatre when it went up. I've been staying with... you know...

A beat.

Funny. All the cases, and... you know. Comes to this.

WATSON　　　　　Mmm.

MRS. HUDSON   I wish you'd never gone after them plans.

WATSON turns to face MRS. HUDSON.

How it started, isn't it?

WATSON   Will you come back? If it can be put right.

MRS. HUDSON   Here?

WATSON   It's your home.

MRS. HUDSON   Well... Mr. Holmes... *(made it feel like home)*

WATSON nods. A beat.

I mean, I *would* stay. If I thought he... if I thought...

A beat.

You know.

WATSON   Of course.

A beat.

MRS. HUDSON   He definitely... didn't...

WATSON shakes his head again. A beat.

Oh dear.

A very tearful MRS. HUDSON exits. WATSON sits at his desk then turns to the audience and says:

WATSON	*(To audience)* The Hunt for Moriarty. A Sherlock Holmes mystery, by Dr. John Watson.

Lights.

It was a grim Wednesday in February, in the year 1900.

HOLMES enters, positioning himself at the window exactly as WATSON himself had been doing.

HOLMES	Fog.
WATSON	*(To audience)* A greasy yellow-brown swirl was setting in for its fourth day, and my friend's restlessness was scaling new heights.
HOLMES	Fog, Watson.
WATSON	*(To audience)* It was two months before the end.
HOLMES	Fog!
WATSON	Do try to settle down.

HOLMES stares determinedly out of the window, as if willing a case to come to him. He is frustrated by the lack of opportunity. WATSON looks at the newspaper.

HOLMES	Nothing of interest in the paper, I suppose.

WATSON	"War rumbles on in Africa..." detail about Bloody Sunday... "Further protests of innocence by sacked War Office Advisor Thomas Beattie..."

HOLMES looks at WATSON.

HOLMES	Of *criminal* interest.

WATSON looks back down at the paper.

WATSON	There have, it seems, been numerous petty thefts.

HOLMES snorts contemptuously.

HOLMES	Look out of this window. Look at it! The robber or the murderer could roam as freely as the tiger does the jungle, and all you have for me is petty theft?
WATSON	I'm not sure what you want.
HOLMES	The London criminal is a dull fellow.
WATSON	He'll be sad to hear that.

Watson bangs on the floor three times with his cane – a signal for MRS. HUDSON.

HOLMES	It's well they don't have days of fog in the Latin countries – the lands of assassination.
WATSON	It's murder you're after then.
HOLMES	It's something to get my teeth into!

WATSON   Have a scone.

MRS. HUDSON enters.

MRS. HUDSON   At this time?

WATSON looks at MRS. HUDSON and shakes his head.

HOLMES   I want someone who might pit their wits against my own. Someone with will. Elan.

WATSON   Elan?

HOLMES   Elan! Panache! A brain, Watson. A scheming, logical mind.

WATSON   Like the Professor?

HOLMES   Ex-professor.

WATSON   Ex-professor.

MRS. HUDSON   Who?

HOLMES   Not him specifically, but... yes.

WATSON   Moriarty's gone, Holmes.

HOLMES   Never. He's just retreated.

WATSON   The world has you to thank for that.

HOLMES   Then the world has stopped watching.

MRS. HUDSON   Who's this Moriarty then?

WATSON   A criminal.

HOLMES   A criminal *mastermind*, Mrs. Hudson. A fearsome and relentless adversary. The spider at the centre of a particularly deadly web.

WATSON   A web that you successfully dismantled some time ago.

HOLMES   Don't be naïve, Watson. Professor Moriarty sits at his game board even now. Readying himself. Planning his next move...

MRS. HUDSON   Sounds like you miss him.

HOLMES   I miss... the challenge. Nothing more.

WATSON   Be patient. There'll be something.

HOLMES   Something more than petty theft, I hope! Petty theft. This stage is set for more than petty theft. Gah!

With that, HOLMES sweeps past WATSON...

WATSON   Where are you going?

...and out of the room. MRS. HUDSDON and WATSON look at each other.

BOTH   *(Together)* Violin.

WATSON   Have you...?

MRS. HUDSON	Top of my wardrobe behind the trunk.
HOLMES	*(Off)* Of all the... Mrs. Hudson?
MRS. HUDSON	Peaceful at your house, is it?
WATSON	Mary and I do engage in lively debate from time to time.
MRS. HUDSON	No stringed instruments then?
HOLMES	*(Off)* Mrs. Hudson!
MRS. HUDSON	Back in a tick...

MRS. HUDSON exits. WATSON turns to the audience.

WATSON	*(To audience)* I was, at that time, living with my dear wife in a terraced row just off Cavendish Square. I had returned to civil practice, though when work took me past Baker Street... or when I missed my friend... I would return to the lodgings we shared, slipping into both armchair and routine like a pair of comfortable shoes.
HOLMES	*(Off)* It's not in the pantry! I've looked!
WATSON	*(To audience)* From time to time when work was slack – or on those occasions when Mary headed north

to visit friends – I would accept Holmes' invitation to take my old room and once more assist him on his fascinating adventures.

HOLMES   *(Off)* Blessed thing seems to have a mind of its own!

MRS. HUDSON   *(Off)* Doesn't it just...?

WATSON   *(To audience)* Of course, when there was no problem for him he split his time more or less evenly between chemical experiments, atonal violin recitals and cocaine. The latter was preferable, the former unpalatable, and as for the violin...

HOLMES enters holding a violin and bow.

HOLMES   A-ha!

WATSON   *(To audience)*   Oh dear.

HOLMES swipes the bow through the air a couple of times, as a fencing master might take practice swings with a foil.

HOLMES   I wonder, Watson, if you are aware of the Sumatran musical form, Malay pantun.

WATSON   I am not.

HOLMES   Then allow me...

14

HOLMES is all set to begin when MRS. HUDSON enters.

MRS. HUDSON   Telegram for you, sir!

HOLMES   Set it down, Mrs. Hudson.

MRS. HUDSON   It sounds important.

HOLMES   It can wait. Now...

The bow almost reaches the strings... but MRS. HUDSON saves the day with a final:

MRS. HUDSON   It's from your brother!

HOLMES is still for a moment, then nods at MRS. HUDSON, who reads aloud:

> *(Reading)* Must see you over Cadogan-West. Coming at once. Mycroft.

HOLMES lowers the bow. WATSON and MRS. HUDSON breathe a sigh of relief.

HOLMES   Brother Mycroft coming here. Well, well. A planet might as well leave its orbit.

WATSON   He's been here before, surely.

HOLMES   Once only. My brother's route is as fixed as a tram car – his Pall Mall lodgings, the Diogenes Club and Whitehall. It must have taken something rather special to derail that. *(To MRS. HUDSON)* Do send him up when he gets here.

MRS. HUDSON   Very good, sir.

HOLMES   Oh, and –

HOLMES holds out the violin and bow. MRS. HUDSON swaps it for the telegram.

A better hiding place next time, I think.

MRS. HUDSON exits.

Cadogan-West. What's that, I wonder? Something governmental, no doubt.

WATSON   What makes you say that?

HOLMES   Because of the unique position Mycroft holds.

WATSON   He's under the British government, isn't he?

HOLMES   In a sense... though it is equally accurate to describe him, at times, as *being* the British government.

WATSON   I don't follow.

HOLMES   My brother has the tidiest and most orderly brain, with the greatest capacity for storing facts, of any man living. The same faculties which I use for the detection of crime, he applies to his ability... and has thus made himself indispensable in the high corridors of power.

WATSON   My word!

HOLMES   The conclusions of every department are passed to him. Each ministry has its specialists, but Mycroft's specialism is omniscience. Again and again his word has decided the national policy.

WATSON   Why don't I know this?

HOLMES   Few outside of government do. Can you imagine the scandal? Not to mention the danger.

A beat. HOLMES has heard something.

Ah! Here he is now. And accompanied by two men. Lestrade is one...

WATSON   No doubt. Even *I* can smell that hair tonic.

HOLMES   The other is a government specialist.

WATSON   How could you possibly know that?

HOLMES   They follow my brother like he's the Pied Piper of Hamelin. Observe...

MYCROFT enters, followed by LESTRADE and a younger, smartly dressed gentleman with an eye-patch, DeWILDE.

Inspector. Brother Mycroft.

MYCROFT   Good morning, Sherlock. This is Sir James deWilde, he's...

DeWILDE   I work for the government.

HOLMES looks at WATSON, who nods in deference to HOLMES' knowledge.

HOLMES   *(To DeWILDE)* This is my associate...

DeWILDE   Dr. Watson, yes. *(To WATSON)* I replaced an old school friend of yours in the foreign office for a time. Percy Phelps?

WATSON   My word! Dear Percy! Of course! That would be...

HOLMES   April last year. The incident with the missing Naval treaty.

DeWILDE   Just so. Bad business. Not Phelps' fault either, as I understand.

WATSON   No harm done – Percy got his job back once Holmes cleared his name.

DeWILDE   True, but I rather think I got a promotion intended for him.

WATSON	I'm sure you earned it; however it came to you.
DeWILDE	Most kind.
HOLMES	How was your walking trip?
DeWILDE	*(Puzzled)* Fine...
HOLMES	You've been back in London less than a week?
DeWILDE	I returned two days ago, yes. How did you know?
LESTRADE	Here we go.
HOLMES	The same way I know you have spent time overseas, most recently in South Africa, have a military background, you speak a range of languages and hail originally from the county of Derbyshire.
DeWILDE	Remarkable! *(To MYCROFT)* You were right.
MYCROFT	*(To HOLMES)* Yes, yes, can we press on? You can show off later.
HOLMES	As you wish.
MYCROFT	*(To LESTRADE)* The floor is yours, Inspector

LESTRADE stands.

LESTRADE	Gentlemen, as reported in the morning's papers, early yesterday morning the body of one Arthur Cadogan-West, Junior Clerk at the Woolwich Arsenal, was found on the train lines just outside Aldgate station on the Underground system.
WATSON	Not come across that story, I'm afraid.
HOLMES	Too busy scouring for petty thefts, no doubt.

HOLMES and WATSON look at one another.

LESTRADE	It was first assumed the man had killed himself. He'd not been robbed; there was no evidence of violence in the carriage...
DeWILDE	However, further... complications... made it necessary to request that Scotland Yard look at the incident more closely.

HOLMES sits.

HOLMES	*(To LESTRADE)* Let us have the facts.
LESTRADE	Cadogan-West left Woolwich suddenly on Monday night. Was last seen by his fiancée, a Miss Violet Westbury, whom he left abruptly in

the fog at 7.30 that evening. Next they heard of him was when his dead body was discovered by a platelayer, six o'clock yesterday morning.

HOLMES Where *precisely* was the body found?

LESTRADE Lying wide of the metals, left hand side of the track as one goes eastward at a point where the line emerges from the tunnel.

WATSON Any injuries?

LESTRADE The head was badly crushed, though that could have come from the fall.

DeWILDE Cadogan-West's record at the Arsenal is good; he's worked there ten years, no cause to suspect foul play, but... there were certain technical papers upon his person...

HOLMES Now we get to the nub of it.

MYCROFT What do you know of the Bruce-Partington submarine, Sherlock?

HOLMES Little more than the name.

MYCROFT It is the most jealously guarded of all government secrets. The Bruce-Partington submarine will change the face of Naval warfare as we know it.

DeWILDE	The plans are kept in an elaborate safe in an office adjoining the arsenal. Under no circumstances were they to be taken from there.
LESTRADE	And yet they were found in the pocket of a dead junior clerk.
WATSON	*Those* were the papers found on Cadogan-West?
DeWILDE	They were.
HOLMES	And now they're recovered?
MYCROFT	No, Sherlock! That's the pinch. Ten papers were taken from Woolwich. There were seven in the pocket of our clerk.
DeWILDE	The three most essential are gone.
MYCROFT	I've never seen the Prime Minister so upset. The Admiralty's in uproar.
LESTRADE	Bound to be.
MYCROFT	Britain has her enemies, brother. We are engaged in a costly war in Southern Africa; one which we are losing...
DeWILDE	Our fleet is providing what support it can from the coast but if those plans fall into the hands of a power who wish to ally with the Boers, however

	temporarily, we will be wiped out at sea and the war might draw on into another year, and another...
MYCROFT	Sir James, do give him the list.

DeWILDE produces a sheet of paper which he hands to HOLMES.

	More than that, with our fleet thus decimated, should that power decide to turn independently toward *our* shores...
HOLMES	I see.

HOLMES looks at the list.

	What's this?
DeWILDE	Contacts at Woolwich, addresses, details... that sort of thing.
MYCROFT	Drop everything, Sherlock. This is a vital international problem. Why did Cadogan-West take the papers? Where are the missing ones? How did he die, how did his body end up where it was found... how can the evil be set right? Answer those questions and you might well see your name on the next honours list.
HOLMES	I have no interest in honours. I play the game for the game's own sake.

HOLMES smiles. He hands the sheet of paper to WATSON.

But it is an interesting problem, and I shall be pleased to look into it. Watson?

WATSON   Yes?

HOLMES   I have a number of telegrams to send this morning. Afterwards I wonder if I might prevail upon you to accompany me. You too, Lestrade.

WATSON   To the Woolwich Arsenal?

HOLMES   Later. First, let's take a trip to Aldgate station. See what we can see...

Music. The stage is reconfigured. WATSON turns to the audience.

WATSON   *(To audience)* Like that, my friend was himself again – the spark dancing in his eyes, the focus returned in full. An hour later he, Lestrade and I stood upon the Underground railroad where it emerges from the tunnel at Aldgate. It was cold, it was damp, a weak grey light stretched thinly through the pall... and Sherlock Holmes was in his element.

HOLMES enters with LESTRADE. There is the distant sound of a train rumbling by.

HOLMES	How long have we got, Inspector?
LESTRADE	Ten minutes, more or less. That's all the railway company can allow. After that this part of the track becomes as busy as Piccadilly Circus.
HOLMES	Then we'd better work quickly. According to your investigation, there was no train ticket found on Cadogan-West's body.
LESTRADE	No indeed. Two tickets for the Woolwich theatre that night, but none for the train.
HOLMES	Curious, as one cannot reach the platform without one. Watch your footing, Watson, these criss-crossing lines are rather treacherous.
WATSON	I'm fine. *(To LESTRADE)* Could he –

WATSON almost trips. Steadies himself. Another train sound. Further away.

	Could he have reached the line by some other means?
LESTRADE	We looked at other approaches, but again, the guard at the barrier would have prevented all access.
WATSON	Do you have a time when the incident occurred?

LESTRADE	An approximate. A passenger passing through Aldgate at around 11.50 Monday night said he heard a heavy thud just before his train reached the station.
WATSON	Did he see anything?
LESTRADE	It was dark of course, and what with the fog and all, but considering where the body was found...
HOLMES	So... the man, dead or alive, either fell or was thrown from the train at some time close to midnight.

HOLMES himself almost slips, then regains his composure.

	Continue.
LESTRADE	The next confusion we have is one of location. London Bridge Station would be Cadogan-West's route to and from Woolwich, and we're way past London Bridge here.
WATSON	That's simple enough – Cadogan-West was engaged in conversation with someone on the train. Missed his stop. Perhaps there was an argument. He tried to leave the carriage, fell out on the line and met his end.

They all take a step back. The sound of a train shuttling past; this one far louder.

HOLMES   And yet, Lestrade, you say he had two tickets for the Woolwich theatre.

LESTRADE   Correct.

HOLMES   If he had intended to convey those papers to London to sell them to a foreign agent, would it not follow that he would have kept the evening clear?

WATSON   The theatre tickets could be a false trail...

HOLMES   Possibly. But consider this – in order to escape detection, Cadogan-West would need to allow this agent to copy all ten papers and *then* return them, *intact*, by morning. He's three short. And apparently wasn't paid for his treason.

WATSON   By Jove, you're right! There ought to have been a substantial sum on his person.

Another distant train.

LESTRADE   All right, how about this? He took the papers to sell them, like you say. Met the agent. They couldn't agree as to price. He boarded the train to

	go home, but the agent followed him, murdered him on the train, took the more essential papers and threw his body from the carriage.
WATSON	Boarded the train without a ticket?
LESTRADE	The agent took it. To prevent anyone discovering where he got on.
HOLMES	Good Lestrade. Your theory holds together, but if all that is true, the case is at an end. The traitor is dead, the papers stolen, and Bruce-Partington submarines will soon be a part of some foreign navy.
LESTRADE	What's your point?
HOLMES	My point, dear Inspector... my... my *point...*

HOLMES tails off, staring down at the tracks.

	(To himself) Could it be that simple...?
WATSON	What is it, Holmes?

A pair of voices disturb the scene, and VIOLET – Cadogan-West's widow – enters, followed by a RAIL OFFICER.

RAIL OFFICER	Madam, please!
VIOLET	Mr. Holmes?

RAIL OFFICER	This is a prohibited area!
VIOLET	Is it you, sir?

WATSON intercepts VIOLET.

WATSON	Are you quite all right, miss?
VIOLET	I need to speak with Mr. Holmes. He's the only one who can help!
RAIL OFFICER	*(To LESTRADE)* Inspector...?
LESTRADE	Madam, if you wouldn't mind...
WATSON	Help with what?
VIOLET	Clearing my Arthur's name!
RAIL OFFICER	Arthur? Who's Arthur?

HOLMES turns, brought instantly out of his reverie.

HOLMES	Cadogan-West. Which would make you Miss Violet Westbury.

VIOLET nods. HOLMES turns to the RAIL OFFICER.

	(To RAIL OFFICER) Do let her through.
RAIL OFFICER	Most irregular.
HOLMES	What brings you here, Miss?
VIOLET	I've been here or hereabouts since yesterday. I can't settle. Can't rest. When they said what my Arthur was

accused of, I knew someone would come. I thought I might be able to have a word with the policeman in charge...

LESTRADE   Oh; well...

VIOLET   But knowing you're here is much better.

LESTRADE   Right.

LESTRADE almost loses his footing on the rails.

VIOLET   Arthur was the most patriotic man upon the earth, Mr. Holmes sir. He'd have cut his right hand off before selling a state secret.

HOLMES   How then do you explain the papers in his possession?

VIOLET   I can't.

HOLMES   Was he in want of any money?

VIOLET   No. We'd plenty saved. We were planning to marry.

HOLMES   Any changes in character in the days leading up to his death?

VIOLET   I... yes.

RAIL OFFICER   Really, Mr. Holmes, I must insist.

Another distant train rumble.

HOLMES	*(To VIOLET)* Quickly now Miss Westbury – speak frankly with me.
VIOLET	I could tell he's been worried, all this last week – he's been saying for a while that security's been slack at work. That it'd be easy for a, a traitor to get anything he likes.
RAIL OFFICER	That's quite enough now.
HOLMES	One moment more, please. *(To VIOLET)* Tell us of Monday evening.
VIOLET	We were to go to the theatre. The fog was so thick that a cab was useless. We walked, and our way took us past his office. Suddenly, he darted away into the fog.
HOLMES	Without a word?
VIOLET	He made a, a kind of gasp, but nothing more. I waited, but he never returned. So I, I walked home, and... and then... came the news... the awful news...

VIOLET starts to break down.

HOLMES	Very well then. Thank you, Miss Westbury.
VIOLET	Save his honour, sir. Please. It was everything to him.

31

RAIL OFFICER	That's enough now miss. *(To LESTRADE)* You'll have to clear the line very soon, Inspector.
LESTRADE	Understood.
HOLMES	*(To RAIL OFFICER)* One question for you sir, if I may.
RAIL OFFICER	Quickly.
HOLMES	I suppose there are no great number of points on a system such as this?
RAIL OFFICER	A few...
HOLMES	A curve, too. Points... and a curve. My word.

Another train rattles by; this one closer. HOLMES watches it pass.

	And there again, look. Cambered roof... with no guard rail...
WATSON	What is it, Holmes? Have you a clue?
HOLMES	An idea, nothing more.
RAIL OFFICER	Unless you want to be flattened by the 2.54 from Uxbridge I suggest you have your idea somewhere else. *(To VIOLET)* This way, miss.

The RAIL OFFICER escorts VIOLET off.

HOLMES	*(To LESTRADE)* Lestrade, you said there was a considerable wound on the body.
LESTRADE	The skull. Yes. Crushed.
HOLMES	A crushed skull? With no traces of blood either in the carriage or here on the tracks? Watson?
WATSON	Unlikely. A head wound forcible enough to crush a skull would have left a surfeit of evidence.
LESTRADE	Do I detect a theory, Mr. Holmes?
HOLMES	There is possibly some light in this darkness, yes... though it may yet flicker out. Inspector, thank you for your time. Let us clear these lines before we're killed. Watson, we'll stay at the station and pick up tickets. We're bound for Woolwich!

Music. The stage is reconfigured.

WATSON	*(To audience)* Once seated on the train Holmes and I talked through the sheet of paper given to us by deWilde. There were two copies of the key that opened the locked room where the plans were secured. A senior clerk named Johnson held one, with the other kept by the official guardian of the papers –

government expert Sir Jonas Walter. His residence was our first port of call – a fine villa with green lawns stretching down to the Thames. We were shown into a sitting room by a silent and rather distressed-looking maid, and before long received our next surprise...

Lights. WATSON and HOLMES stand as if looking out of a window.

HOLMES   From what I understand of Sir Jonas, I fully expected him to greet us himself. Something is quite wrong here.

WATSON   According to deWilde's notes, he was away from Woolwich from Monday afternoon onward.

HOLMES   Visiting Admiral Sinclair, yes.

WATSON   You don't suppose he and the Admiral are behind this business.

HOLMES   I do not.

WATSON   It might account for the atmosphere.

HOLMES   My dear Watson, Sir Jonas' reputation is flawless, and well-earned. As for the Admiral, if *he's* taken to stealing plans we're all doomed.

After a moment they are joined by COL. WALTER, brother of Sir Jonas. He is holding a large snifter of brandy and appears to be in some distress.

COL. WALTER   I'm sorry if... er... to, to keep you waiting. I'm Colonel Walter. Valentine. I'm... Jonas' brother.

HOLMES   Pleasure to meet you. Sherlock Holmes.

WATSON   Doctor John Watson.

COL. WALTER   Please, do sit. If. Or. Or stand. Whatever you prefer.

He takes a plentiful swallow at the snifter.

WATSON   Is this a bad time?

A beat. COL. WALTER looks at them strangely.

COL. WALTER   You don't know? The butler has his instructions – he was to inform visitors on arrival –

HOLMES   We were shown in by a maid, not a butler.

COL. WALTER   I see.

He takes a moment to compose himself.

Well. The truth of the matter is... my brother Jonas is dead.

WATSON   Good Lord.

COL. WALTER	He died this morning.
WATSON	I'm most dreadfully sorry.
COL. WALTER	Yes. Well. He was, ah...

He finishes his brandy.

	It's this horrible scandal. This... theft. My brother was a man of very sensitive honour, and it would appear... it would appear to have broken his heart...
HOLMES	We had hoped he might help us clear the matter up.
COL. WALTER	It was as much a mystery to him as to all of us. He spent most of yesterday in here with the police. Naturally he believed Cadogan-West to be guilty, but the rest? Inconceivable.
HOLMES	You yourself cannot throw any light on the affair?
COL. WALTER	I know only what my brother told me.
HOLMES	Which was?
COL. WALTER	Well, that this, this Partington business lends weight to a common theory about a leak. A leak in government. And he... he was so proud of his record at Woolwich...

forgive me, gentlemen; I don't wish to be discourteous, but you can understand, this is quite the blow...

HOLMES   Our condolences.

COL. WALTER   The butler will show you out.

COL. WALTER exits. A beat.

HOLMES   Interesting.

WATSON   Interesting?

HOLMES   And suggestive.

WATSON   A man is heartbroken and you consider that interesting and suggestive?

HOLMES   No... I consider the fact that Valentine has been living here interesting... the theory about a leak is suggestive.

WATSON   You don't know he's been living here.

HOLMES   About a month would be my estimate.

WATSON   How?

HOLMES   Those were not his carpet slippers – he takes a half-size larger. The jacket was similarly ill-fitting, and that Charles de Squeyre Armagnac too casually drunk for an infrequent visitor.

WATSON   What does it matter?

HOLMES   It possibly doesn't. Doesn't stop it being interesting.

WATSON   You really are the most peculiar man.

HOLMES   Be that as it may, we've learned all we can here. Let's return to Baker Street. I must get a communication to Mycroft.

WATSON checks his pocket watch.

WATSON   At this time?

HOLMES   He has something more I need.

WATSON   Such as?

HOLMES   A list of foreign spies or international agents known to operate in England. With full addresses, naturally.

WATSON   Naturally.

HOLMES   It was the one useful thing missing from deWilde's list... though I *can* understand why it wasn't present. I'll send the irregulars. Tomorrow I shall run errands. You have places to go.

WATSON	Do I indeed?
HOLMES	Firstly, you'll interview the senior cl erk at the Woolwich Arsenal.
WATSON	A mister... *(Consulting DeWILDE's list)* Sidney Johnson. Then?
HOLMES	Head to the Diogenes Club. Meet my brother... and get his list.

Music.

WATSON *(To audience)* Sidney Johnson, the nervous-looking senior clerk, met me at the office. He told me that in order to get to the plans, Cadogan-West would have needed three keys – one for the outer door, the second for the office, and the last for the safe itself – the late Sir Jonas Walter was the only man in possession of all three. So, did Cadogan-West – a man Johnson trusted as high as anyone in the office – steal those keys? And how? Was there more to Sir Jonas' death than met the eye...?

A beat.

And so... to the Diogenes Club.

The stage is reconfigured. Chairs are placed at the back of the space, with ACTORS FOUR & FIVE

sitting in them, reading newspapers or periodicals.
MYCROFT is in another initially.

There are many in London who, whether through shyness or misanthropy, have no wish for the company of their fellow man... and yet who, at the same time, enjoy comfortable chairs, fine whisky and the latest periodicals. It is for those singular individuals that the Diogenes Club exists.

ACTORS look up and loudly shush WATSON.

It is patronised and populated by the most unsociable men one could ever hope not to meet. No member is permitted to take the least notice of any other one, and only in the Stranger's Room is talking permitted.

Another shush.

It was in here that I met with Mycroft.

Lights. MYCROFT moves forward and joins WATSON.

MYCROFT   My brother has you scurrying round after him again, does he?

WATSON   I don't mind.

MYCROFT	Ha! Rather you than me. Give me a problem I can solve from an armchair and I'll present you with a credible solution in half no time, but running here, and running there, questioning maids and whatnot, lying on my face with a magnifying glass to my eye? Not my *métier*.

He takes an envelope from his jacket.

	The list, as requested. Though do please tell Sherlock, charmed as I was to see his urchins last night, that I *am* somewhat stretched at present. If intelligence is required, deWilde's his man.
WATSON	Oh, I think he rather thought that your access might... *(be greater)*
MYCROFT	Yes, yes, of course I have access – but deWilde's *specialty* is intelligence.
WATSON	I thought he was in the foreign office.
MYCROFT	He *was*. Promoted to the War Office last October under that officious pen-pusher, Fitzmaurice.
WATSON	He did mention a promotion.
MYCROFT	He's a rising star. Has been ever since his return from the Transvaal.

WATSON	Was he part of the war?
MYCROFT	In a sense. He'd been working undercover as a Boer scout for years prior to the commencement, feeding us intelligence until mid '97. Has a fair claim to some of the gold there, too.
WATSON	What happened in '97?
MYCROFT	Lost the use of his eye. Returned to London. And high time.
WATSON	What does that mean?
MYCROFT	Secretary of State Henry Petty-Fitzmaurice is out of his depth. Everyone knows it. The War Department needs someone with a head for strategy. Someone who can see problems almost before they raise their heads.
WATSON	And Sir James is that man?
MYCROFT	I should say so. He's worked in every corner of the world, had a dozen different identities...
WATSON	I would never have known.
MYCROFT	He wouldn't have been doing his job properly if you had. I daresay that's why Sherlock asked for *my* help instead of his.

WATSON	I'm not sure I follow.
MYCROFT	Doctor, you have to know my brother very well to recognise when he feels threatened intellectually.
WATSON	Does he?
MYCROFT	He can pass it off as admiration, dismiss it as nonsense, but mark me, Sir James deWilde has ruffled brother Sherlock's feathers. It was the same with that Professor you fenced with, what was it...?
WATSON	Moriarty.
MYCROFT	That's the one. And the... oh; she outwitted him with the photograph... I almost had it... ah...
WATSON	Irene Adler. "The Woman."
MYCROFT	There. You see? "The Professor." "The Woman." The moment Sir James is given a soubriquet, you'll know he's gotten under Sherlock's skin. Now, off with you. You're too effusive for a place like this. Wish Sherlock well. Tell him I'll deal with the other matters later.

MYCROFT heads for his chair.

WATSON	What other matters?

MYCROFT does not answer, instead reaching his seat and lifting his newspaper.

Mycroft? What other matters?

Another shush. Music. The stage is reconfigured. We are back at Baker Street.

(To audience) By that evening the fog had begun to lift a little and Baker Street, for days a series of dark angles rising from the yellowed mist, was now washed in pale, watery sunlight. I arrived in our study to find Holmes and Mrs. Hudson together in silent concentration, surrounded by maps and reference books...

Lights. HOLMES has a large map spread across the table. MRS. HUDSON stands next to him, studying it just as keenly as the detective himself.

HOLMES   Ah! There you are. Did brother Mycroft come through?

WATSON   He did.

HOLMES   Excellent.

MRS. HUDSON puts her hand out. After a beat, WATSON gives the list to her.

Now... let us see... *(To MRS. HUDSON)* Mrs. Hudson, if you will...

MRS. HUDSON	There's five names on this here list... one of them's marked "missing," another might well be in Paris... that leaves us with three.
HOLMES	The first, please?
MRS. HUDSON	*(Reading)* Adolphus Meyer, six Great George Street, Westminster.
HOLMES	Very well...

HOLMES starts to inspect the map, cross-referencing it with a copy of Bradshaw and other papers thrown across the table.

WATSON	What's going on?
MRS. HUDSON	Mr. Holmes is testing a theory.
WATSON	What about?
MRS. HUDSON	Why there was no train ticket on the clerk's body.
WATSON	Know all about the affair now, do you?
MRS. HUDSON	I've always known. Not as if you whisper when your little friends come calling.
WATSON	They're not our "little friends," they're – *(Holmes' clients)*
HOLMES	No. No good. Next!

MRS. HUDSON	*(Consulting the list)* Next... Louis LaRotière. Campden Mansions, Notting Hill.
HOLMES	Notting Hill...

HOLMES' head is back down to the map and the papers.

WATSON	And this cross-referencing is....?
MRS. HUDSON	*(Proudly)* ...my idea.
WATSON	*Yours?*
HOLMES	Don't be so dismissive, Watson...
WATSON	Go on then.
MRS. HUDSON	Mr. Holmes was speculating as to how he thought the body might have ended up on the line. I happened to say as how, when I travelled on the Underground, which I used to do with Mr. Hudson from time to time –
HOLMES	No. Next!
MRS. HUDSON	*(Reading)* Hugo Oberstein. Thirteen Caulfield Gardens, Kensington.
HOLMES	Carry on.

HOLMES is back at the charts.

MRS. HUDSON	Right, well, whenever the trains run clear of the tunnels, there are points

where you can see windows right above your head. And I can remember Mr. Hudson saying to me on more than one occasion, fancy having a train below your window. What a din!

WATSON   What has that got to do with this business?

HOLMES slaps the table in triumph.

HOLMES   Everything! It has everything to do with it!

He moves away from the table and approaches WATSON. MRS. HUDSON picks up HOLMES' magnifying glass and looks at the map.

He was on the train.

WATSON   That's nothing new.

HOLMES   Not on it. *On* it.

WATSON   You've lost me.

HOLMES   It came to me at Aldgate, when we looked at the points and the curvature of the line just before the station. Our Mr. Cadogan-West had no train ticket because he never boarded. His *body* was on the *roof.* Placed there from the window of...

HOLMES waits and defers to MRS. HUDSON.

MRS. HUDSON   Me?

HOLMES nods.

                    ...one of these here apartments,
                    overlooking the line.

MRS. HUDSON smiles with satisfaction.

WATSON   So he didn't die from the fall?

HOLMES   Indeed not. The poor fellow was
                    dead already.

WATSON   And a body wouldn't simply stay
                    put?

HOLMES   The roof of a Metropolitan train is
                    rounded, with no rails. So much was
                    observed yesterday. If a train jolts,
                    say, or there is less uniformity to its
                    movement...

WATSON   *(Beginning to get it)* Like when it
                    rides points or takes a curve...

HOLMES   ...then something on the roof is likely
                    to slide off.

WATSON   Holmes, that's brilliant!

HOLMES   It was Mrs. Hudson's detail that
                    provided the brilliance.

MRS. HUDSON   I'll let dear Mr. Hudson take that
                    one, God rest him.

HOLMES	Arthur Cadogan-West was no thief. On the contrary, he became mixed up in this business – and lost his life – trying to stop one.
WATSON	Who?
HOLMES	That, for the time being, is less clear, but we now know where the thief intended to take the stolen plans...

HOLMES looks at MRS. HUDSON once more.

MRS. HUDSON	Me again?
HOLMES	Oh yes.
MRS. HUDSON	*(Proudly)* To Hugo Oberstein. Caulfield Gardens, Kensington.
HOLMES	Come, Watson! There's not a moment to lose.
WATSON	Now?
HOLMES	Now. And bring a jemmy. And a chisel. We'll need to force a window.
WATSON	You don't expect the fellow to be within?
HOLMES	I do not. If he's not on the continent lining up international buyers already he doesn't deserve to be on Mycroft's list.
WATSON	Then what can we do?

HOLMES	Search the fellow's apartment. Find a way to draw him back before he makes a sale...

Music. The stage is reconfigured. WATSON turns to the audience.

WATSON	*(To audience)* Holmes was right of course; Oberstein was not at home. He and I spent hours combing the dingy, cluttered rooms looking for anything that might aid us in our retrieval...

HOLMES enters with a pile of books. He places them down.

	(To HOLMES) Nothing through there?

HOLMES	Hand-written calculations about depth and pressure but nothing of consequence.

WATSON	That's proof, isn't it?

HOLMES	It's suggestive, but unhelpful. Look through those, would you?

HOLMES strides past WATSON.

	I'm heading to the kitchen.

HOLMES exits.

WATSON	*(To audience)* The apartment did indeed look out over the train line...

with trains slowing to a stop on more than one occasion just outside. Inspecting the living room window, dark rosettes of blood flecked both the carpet below and the sill itself.

HOLMES returns with a tin. He works at the lid with a small chisel. WATSON starts looking through the books.

(To HOLMES) I don't know how you do it Holmes, I really don't. Putting things together as you do.

HOLMES   Observation and deduction.

WATSON   I could never apply myself to your extent.

HOLMES   Doesn't mean you lack the skills. Anything?

WATSON   Historical biographies. No page notes.

HOLMES   Herr Oberstein has been very thorough in covering his tracks. It's this tin or nothing. While I work it, go through our timeline again. Good practice for you.

WATSON   Very well... Cadogan-West suspected all was not right at Woolwich. Voiced his concerns to his fiancée –

HOLMES	Obliquely...
WATSON	...but enough for her to notice. Monday, he sees something or someone out of place at work... it rouses suspicion in the man...
HOLMES	Then?
WATSON	The day ends; he meets his fiancée and they walk to the theatre.
HOLMES	The walk takes them back past the Arsenal...
WATSON	...and Cadogan-West sees this suspicious someone leaving the office with the plans. Without another word he abandons Miss Westbury and pursues this person...
HOLMES	The fog providing ample cover...
WATSON	Arrives at this very house, tries to interrupt the transaction, is killed...
HOLMES	And his body?
WATSON	Placed on the roof of a slow-moving train as it edges down the line.
HOLMES	But not before...?
WATSON	Not before they place seven of the ten pages of the Bruce-Partington plans on Cadogan-West's body, thus implicating him in the theft.

HOLMES   *(Prying the lid)* That... is... it!

With a jerk, the lid of the box springs open.

What's this, Watson? Eh? What's this?

HOLMES holds up a sheaf of newspaper clippings.

A slip, Herr Oberstein! And you were doing so well!

WATSON   What do you have there?

HOLMES   See for yourself.

He passes a clipping over to WATSON.

WATSON   Newspaper clipping? The *Telegraph*... agony column.

HOLMES   Look at the message in the top right-hand corner...

WATSON   *(Reading)* "Hoped to hear sooner. Terms agreed to. Write fully to address given on card. Pierrot."

HOLMES holds up a second.

HOLMES   This one must be next – again, *Daily Telegraph,* agony column, top-right corner, *(Reading)* "Too complex for description. Must have full report. Pierrot." Now we have both form and forum.

WATSON picks up a third clipping.

| WATSON | Pierrot again. Top right. *(Reading)* "Matter presses. Must withdraw offer unless contract completed. Make appointment by letter. Will confirm by advertisement." |

HOLMES holds up the fourth.

| HOLMES | And this one last of all. *(Reading)* "Monday night after nine. Two taps. Only ourselves. Payment in cash when goods delivered. Pierrot." |

| WATSON | Would that be the Monday in question? |

| HOLMES | Certainly. Evidently the thief is a suspicious type. I think we can use that. We shall head to the offices of the *Daily Telegraph* first thing. By Monday night we ought to have brought this matter to a conclusion. |

Music. HOLMES shifts position.

| WATSON | *(To audience)* Amid the waiting that weekend, one significant piece of information came our way – a telegram from Sir James. |

DeWILDE enters and is held in a spotlight.

| DeWILDE | Spot of luck. Thief's papers incomplete. One sheet of returned plans vital for submarine |

construction. May delay any sale or transfer. Happy hunting.

DeWILDE exits.

WATSON   *(To audience)* Holmes took the news with his usual nonchalance but I could see he was pleased. In an instant he had adjusted his strategy, and by Monday night we were ready – Holmes and I, back in Oberstein's flat... though this time with a less-than-comfortable Inspector Lestrade...

LESTRADE enters, pacing. HOLMES is at the window. WATSON in a chair.

LESTRADE   You mean to say that this is the *second* time you've broken in here?

HOLMES   We broke in just the once, Inspector. *This* time we used a key.

LESTRADE   That you found on your first visit. When you broke in!

WATSON   We also found the newspaper clippings. Think more of that.

LESTRADE   And removed them.

WATSON   We did.

LESTRADE   Which is burglary.

WATSON   Ah.

HOLMES	Without those clippings, we wouldn't know we have our man.

LESTRADE shakes his head.

LESTRADE	No wonder you get results that are beyond us, Mr. Holmes. We can't do such as this in the force. But you mark my words...
HOLMES	One day we'll go too far. Yes.
LESTRADE	You're sure this will work?
WATSON	Holmes put the letter in himself. "Tonight. Same hour. Two taps. Most vital – your own safety at stake. Pierrot." It's perfect.
LESTRADE	Still quite a gamble.
HOLMES	It might be the only card we can play, but it is the right one. Our thief is nervous. He'll come. For now, we wait.

Music.

WATSON	*(To audience)* An hour passed, and then another. When the nearby church bell struck eleven I felt all hope was lost... only to see Holmes sit bolt upright and whisper –
HOLMES	He's here. Ready yourselves.

There is the sound of two sharp taps on the door. HOLMES exits. A moment later a figure enters, scarf over his face, hat brim pulled down low. He sees WATSON and LESTRADE and turns. HOLMES is behind him. There is a brief moment of physical resistance, but in vain. The hat and scarf are removed to reveal... COL. WALTER.

COL. WALTER   Let me go! Let me go, damn you!

LESTRADE   Well, well, who's this then?

HOLMES   Inspector Lestrade, allow me to introduce you to Colonel Valentine Walter. Younger brother of the late Sir Jonas Walter, Senior Adviser to Henry Petty-Fitzmaurice, the Secretary of State for War...

WATSON   ...and the man who stole the Bruce-Partington plans.

COL. WALTER   I did nothing of the kind. I'm here to see Mr. Oberstein, nothing more.

HOLMES   Everything is known, Colonel Walter.

COL. WALTER looks at HOLMES and realises the game is up. He sits, defeated.

We know that you were pressed for money. You had given up your own residence and were living with Sir Jonas – providing you ample opportunity to take an impress of the three keys your late brother held. We know you entered into correspondence with Herr Oberstein regarding the sale of the plans. We are aware that you went down to the office on Monday of last week, but that you were seen and followed by Cadogan-West, who left all private concerns and kept at your heels in the fog until you reached this very house. There he intervened, and there it was, Colonel Walter, that to treason you added the more terrible crime of murder!

COL. WALTER   I did not! Before God, I swear I did not!

HOLMES   Tell us, then, how Cadogan-West met his end. And why.

COL. WALTER   A Stock Exchange debt is why. And that damn conman.

LESTRADE   Who's this?

COL. WALTER   I met him at Mendoza's. The boxing rooms by the Stock Exchange?

HOLMES   I know them well.

COL. WALTER   Unusual chap. Singled me out. Said he knew of my trouble and that he had a system. I could make a lot of money... and I *did...* at first. Then the whole thing seemed to just... collapse. Oberstein contacted me, offered me five thousand. Swore I'd never be caught. I wanted to save myself from ruin, that's all.

WATSON   What happened with the clerk?

COL. WALTER   He followed me, as you say – pushed into the room, said I was a traitor – got louder, more furious... then Oberstein struck him.

LESTRADE   With?

COL. WALTER   I didn't see. Something heavy. Don't think he meant to kill him, but I knew by the way he hit the floor – by the way he bled, that...

A beat.

The plan had been to copy the blueprints so I could return them, but with the time we had left... Oberstein had to improvise.

HOLMES   Where is he now?

COL. WALTER   Paris.

HOLMES   You have a way to get in touch with him?

COL. WALTER	By letter to the Hotel du Louvre. Why?
HOLMES	Because reparation might still be within your power.
LESTRADE	Now, Mr. Holmes –
HOLMES	I do not mean to cheat you out of an arrest Inspector, but a little help at the end of this affair might go some way to easing certain consciences.
COL. WALTER	Anything I can.
HOLMES	Then take up pen and paper and write this to Herr Oberstein:

Music. A sequence. As we hear what's in the letter, the stage is reconfigured and we create our next location. This next is recorded, as everyone lends a hand creating the foyer of the Charing Cross Hotel.

Dear Sir – With regard to our transaction, you will no doubt know by now that an essential detail is missing. I have a tracing which will make it complete, though I must ask for a further advance of five hundred pounds for the trouble. This must be paid in person, and here in London – I shall expect to meet you in the smoking room of the Charing Cross Hotel at noon on Saturday. Only English notes or gold will be taken.

During the change, LESTRADE exits with COL. WALTER, plants are brought on, HOLMES and WATSON take their places and watch a particular chair... and eventually OBERSTEIN enters. He has a package with him. He sits and looks around him nervously.

There he is, Watson. Hugo Oberstein in the flesh.

WATSON   Shall we go?

HOLMES   A moment more. I'm trying to place the fellow.

WATSON   You've met him?

HOLMES   Not that I recall, but I've seen the face. Hello... what's this?

A female PORTER approaches OBERSTEIN with a small note on a tray. Bows to him, exits. OBERSTEIN opens it. Reads it, then looks round frantically.

WATSON   Who's he looking for?

The music darkens. OBERSTEIN starts to shake, then convulse. He slides from the chair and onto the floor. We hear recorded voices calling things such as "Are you all right, sir?" "My God, he's having a seizure!" "Somebody help him!" "He's not breathing!" "Give him some room!" and, inevitably, "Is there a Doctor in the house?" WATSON is up and across to the body, now in full spasm. HOLMES

61

goes with him. Despite his best efforts, WATSON is too late.

Somebody better fetch the police. He's dead.

The recorded voices fade.

HOLMES   Poison?

WATSON   Yes, but when? We watched him enter; he didn't ingest anything. The only thing he touched was –

WATSON leans over to pick up the card.

HOLMES   Don't!

HOLMES leans down and smells the card. Short, shallow breaths.

Contact poison. Cyanide base, but with more behind it.

WATSON   I've never seen anything work so quickly.

Using a handkerchief, HOLMES carefully picks up the card.

HOLMES   I shall analyse it. Be a good fellow and fetch that porter, would you? The one who brought Oberstein the note.

WATSON exits. HOLMES gingerly places card and handkerchief in his pocket as WATSON returns with the PORTER.

(To PORTER) Ah, hello there. Might you be able to describe the person who gave you the card for Mr. Oberstein?

PORTER   Older gent he was sir. Wearing a long, black overcoat.

HOLMES   And gloves, I'll wager. Did he speak to you?

PORTER   He did. Then he put the note on my tray and paid me half a crown.

WATSON   Never!

PORTER   Said he was paying me double because the card was really for two men.

HOLMES   Who was the other man?

PORTER   You, sir.

Music.

He pointed you out. Said as how you were Mr. Sherlock Holmes of Baker Street and the note was for the both of you.

Dismissed by HOLMES, the PORTER exits. HOLMES again removes the card carefully from his pocket and unwraps it. This time he reads it.

HOLMES *(Reading)* "The innocent seldom find an uneasy pillow. M."

WATSON Not sure I'd describe Oberstein as innocent.

HOLMES Nor I, though it would seem to be a reference to his death.

WATSON M... for Machiavelli, perhaps?

HOLMES The quote? No – William Cowper. Poet. Died a hundred years ago.

HOLMES looks around him.

It appears we have strayed into a larger game. Worse still, we were expected.

WATSON What does it mean?

A beat.

HOLMES It means, my dear Watson, that Moriarty is in play...

Music. HOLMES exits. The stage is reconfigured and we return to Baker Street.

WATSON *(To audience)* The day after Oberstein's horrible demise, British representatives recovered the missing three pages of the Bruce-Partington plans from a trunk in a Paris hotel room. Notes by the bedside indicated that all the naval centres of Europe were poised and ready to bid. Three days later, we received a visit from an extremely grateful Sir James deWilde...

Lights. HOLMES and DeWILDE enter and shake hands.

DeWILDE   You've done your country a great service and we thank you.

WATSON   Our pleasure.

DeWILDE   Mycroft would have come himself...

HOLMES   No he wouldn't.

DeWILDE smiles.

DeWILDE   Well, with the situation in Siam, civil unrest in a variety of different countries, not to mention the change of strategy in Africa...

HOLMES   Yes, yes, he's very important.

WATSON   I read Lord Kitchener is taking charge of the war effort.

DeWILDE   That's right. I'll be liaising with him directly from now on.

WATSON   Oh?

DeWILDE	Yes, I, ah... Colonel Walter's arrest has left something of a vacuum in the War Office, and the Secretary of State requested... me.
WATSON	Senior Adviser?

DeWILDE nods.

	That's quite a step. Congratulations.
DeWILDE	*(To HOLMES)* I believe your brother gave me the final seal of approval.
HOLMES	Doubtless he'll have had his reasons.
WATSON	Well of course he did! *(To DeWILDE)* Mycroft told me about your background. And your abilities.
DeWILDE	I'm sure he was being generous.
HOLMES	We don't wish to keep you...
DeWILDE	Of course. Thanks again – It's been fascinating seeing you work. Good afternoon, Doctor.

DeWILDE exits. WATSON turns to HOLMES.

WATSON	Holmes, I know that you can be cool at times...
HOLMES	I was direct. Not cool.
WATSON	Hardly a return on Sir James' courtesy.

HOLMES	I have other things on my mind!
WATSON	He didn't *need* to come here.
HOLMES	On that we agree. There *was* no need for his visit, other than to boast about his further advancement. Why would the Professor wish Oberstein dead?
WATSON	Perhaps he's incidental.
HOLMES	Moriarty wastes no moves. If someone dies, it is because *he* wants it.
WATSON	I didn't find him boastful.
HOLMES	The worst kind of boast, Watson, is one couched in humility. *(Signalling WATSON)* Would you?

WATSON knocks three times on the floor with his stick again.

WATSON	Ought we have asked deWilde? About Moriarty?
HOLMES	The "Senior Adviser?" I think not. This is our game alone.
WATSON	Did you just give him a name?
HOLMES	I beg your pardon?
WATSON	Sir James. You gave him a name. A soubriquet.

| **HOLMES** | Why does that matter? |
| **WATSON** | Doesn't really. |

WATSON smiles to himself. MRS. HUDSON enters carrying a dusty box.

| **MRS. HUDSON** | Good timing. I just put my hands on it when you knocked. |

She takes it to the table.

| **WATSON** | What's that? |
| **HOLMES** | Keepsake box. |

HOLMES joins her, taking a small key from his pocket.

| **WATSON** | I had absolutely no idea. |
| **HOLMES** | Of course you hadn't. |

He opens the box and produces a photograph. Looks at it and smiles.

I was right! You see?

| **WATSON** | What about? |
| **HOLMES** | Oberstein. I had seen him before. |

He turns the photograph round and shows it to WATSON.

There.

| **WATSON** | Why do you have a photograph of a spy in your keepsake box? |

HOLMES   The picture is not *of* him. He's in the background.

MRS. HUDSON   Who's this in the foreground?

HOLMES   That, Mrs. Hudson, is "the woman."

WATSON   Soubriquet.

MRS. HUDSON   Sue who?

HOLMES looks at WATSON quizzically, then:

HOLMES   Her name is Irene. Irene Adler...

HOLMES puts the photograph down and walks to his armchair. WATSON moves to MRS. HUDSON.

MRS. HUDSON   Doesn't ring a bell.

WATSON   *(To MRS. HUDSON)* Do you remember Holmes being visited by the King of Bohemia? Came to us, ooh, a couple of years ago with a rather delicate favour to ask...

Lights up on VON ORMSTEIN, an elaborately dressed, worried-looking man. MRS. HUDSON and WATSON watch on.

VON ORMSTEIN   Mr. Holmes, my name is Wilhelm Gottreich Sigismond von Ormstein, Grand Duke of Cassel-Felstein and hereditary King of Bohemia.

HOLMES   I am aware.

VON ORMSTEIN	As you may know, I am about to be married to Clotilde Lothman von Saxe-Meningen, second daughter of the King of Scandinavia.
HOLMES	Congratulations.
VON ORMSTEIN	Her family have strict principles. A shadow of doubt as to my conduct would bring the matter to an end.
HOLMES	Is there such a shadow?
VON ORMSTEIN	Five years ago, during a lengthy visit to Warsaw, I... made the acquaintance... of the well-known adventuress, Irene Adler.

HOLMES finds a book and starts to leaf through it. As he does so:

MRS. HUDSON	Ahhh... *that's* who she is...
HOLMES	*(Consulting book)* Let me see... born in New Jersey in the year 1865... contralto... La Scala... Prima Donna, Imperial Opera of Warsaw. Retired from operatic stage, now living in London.

He shuts the book.

Your Majesty became entangled with this person? Wrote her, I imagine, letters of a compromising nature? Letters you wish returned?

| VON ORMSTEIN | Letters can be dismissed as fakes. It is a photograph I require. She and I together, in... well... |
| HOLMES | In... love? |

VON ORMSTEIN nods.

| VON ORMSTEIN | The affair did not end well. If she should resort to blackmail... |
| HOLMES | You think it likely? |

VON ORMSTEIN lowers his head.

I see.

| VON ORMSTEIN | Mr. Holmes, I implore you – find a way to retrieve that picture. You have carte blanche on expenses. |

HOLMES stands and shakes VON ORMSTEIN's hand.

I'll room at the Savoy.

| HOLMES | I'll be in touch. |

VON ORMSTEIN exits. HOLMES moves to the window. Lights.

MRS. HUDSON	I take it you got the picture.
HOLMES	I did not.
MRS. HUDSON	You're joking.

HOLMES	She outplayed me, Mrs. Hudson. Spotted my ploy, saw through my disguise, knew what I was up to... she is – in a word – magnificent. When I came to retrieve what I thought would be the King's photograph, I instead found a note addressed to me, confessing she intended no blackmail... and an entirely different picture. *That* picture.
WATSON	Adler with Oberstein?
HOLMES	And several others. The photograph was intended for the King.
MRS. HUDSON	How come *you* ended up with it then?
HOLMES	I asked for it. In lieu of fee.
MRS. HUDSON	Happy with that, was he?
HOLMES	Very much so. Said he owed me a favour, in fact.
MRS. HUDSON	All right for some.
WATSON	What are they dressed as?
MRS. HUDSON	Commedia characters.
WATSON	I'm sorry?
MRS. HUDSON	Commedia dell'arte. Type of theatre.

A beat.

> What?

WATSON   Mrs. Hudson, you surprise me!

MRS. HUDSON   Can't think why. I love theatre. I go regular. Commedia was one of my late husband's favourites. There are all these different characters, you see?

She starts to point at the figures in the picture.

> One you're pointing at? That's Pierrot.

WATSON   Pierrot... the name Oberstein used to contact Colonel Walter!

HOLMES nods.

MRS. HUDSON   That one there's Arlechino. Next to him is il Dottore... that's Pantalone there... Scaramuccia... and in the middle, your Miss Adler... as Isabella.

WATSON turns the picture over.

WATSON   *(Reading)* "L'Assemblea dei Furfanti, 1898."

HOLMES   "The Scoundrels' Assembly."

MRS. HUDSON   I've seen that advertised.

HOLMES   Yes?

MRS. HUDSON	Never seen it on anywhere though.
WATSON	It's one of these... comedy... plays then?
HOLMES	So one is led to believe... *(To MRS. HUDSON)* Mrs. Hudson, where would one take in productions such as these?
MRS. HUDSON	Little Theatre. Haymarket. It's the only one as puts Commedia on regular.
HOLMES	Westminster. Of course. Get your hat, Watson.
WATSON	Are we going to see the play?
HOLMES	There is no play.
WATSON	What is it then, this, "Scoundrels' Assembly?"
HOLMES	I believe we're looking at them. And the Little Theatre's where we'll find out more.
WATSON	You can't be serious. This picture's two years old!
HOLMES	The trail might not be fresh but it is there, and I intend to follow it!

Music. The stage is reconfigured. WATSON addresses the audience.

WATSON	*(To audience)* Our arrival at Haymarket that late afternoon coincided with the curtain of a matinee performance. We pushed gently through a crowd of theatregoers and, upon entering the Little Theatre, my first thought was that we should seek out the manager. Holmes, as ever, had a keener idea...

HOLMES enters with Ronald SMITH, the Little Theatre's caretaker.

HOLMES	Watson, I'd like you to meet Ronald Smith. Caretaker.
WATSON	Pleasure to meet you.
SMITH	Likewise.
HOLMES	I was able to assist Mr. Smith some months ago in a small matter involving a racing pigeon.
SMITH	*(Proudly)* Prize winning, thanks to you, sir.
HOLMES	Happy to help. A most absorbing mystery. Now, Watson, Mr. Smith here will check the company are out of the building, and then he will escort us backstage.
SMITH	Your friend wants to come too, does he?

WATSON	If that's all right.
SMITH	Long as you don't scare easy.
HOLMES	Ah yes, Mr. Smith was telling me about the theatre's ghosts.
WATSON	Oh?
SMITH	You might not hear 'em in the day time, but they're there. Like I told Mr. Holmes. Down below. In a store room under the stage.
HOLMES	Sounds fascinating, doesn't it?
WATSON	Oh. Yes. Fascinating.
SMITH	I'll check the coast is clear. Back in a tick.

SMITH exits.

WATSON	Is there anyone in London you *haven't* helped?
HOLMES	Mr. Smith is a happy accident – his fear of the supernatural should afford us some privacy. He doesn't go into the understage areas if he can help it.
WATSON	You really think you're onto something here, don't you?
HOLMES	He spoke of whispered voices, of furniture having been moved... he

even mentioned finding burned fragments of letters in a "funny language," so... yes.

WATSON   And he's never considered it might be one of the actors, say?

HOLMES   The room in which all this occurred has one entrance which remains locked, and to which he has the only key.

SMITH enters carrying a lantern and a large key.

SMITH   It gets quite dark, so...

HOLMES   Too kind.

He hands over the lantern and the key.

SMITH   You'll need this to get in, of course.

HOLMES   Oh, you aren't...?

SMITH   No fear. I'll show you the staircase but that's as far as I go.

HOLMES   Lead on...

Music. The stage is reconfigured. HOLMES and WATSON enter an understage area, clutching the lantern and looking about them. HOLMES sniffs the air.

                       Smell that, Watson?

WATSON   All just smells musty to me. What is this place?

HOLMES	Costume store, prop store... you'll find them in all theatres – though I suspect this particular room has a more gloried past.
WATSON	Oh...?
HOLMES	The pictures on the wall.
WATSON	Not props themselves?
HOLMES	No, no. Originals.
WATSON	My word.

They look around.

	Well. Dead end. Smith's right.
HOLMES	And yet somebody *has* been here within the last two hours. If you couldn't smell it out there, you must be able to now.
WATSON	What?
HOLMES	Smoke.

HOLMES spots something on the floor. He removes his magnifying glass.

	And here – an unbroken line of ash.
WATSON	Good Lord!
HOLMES	It comes most certainly from a Ritmeester cigar. Dutch brand.

WATSON	Smoke in a locked room yes, but cigar ash? How is it possible?
HOLMES	It isn't. Unless we apply the old maxim that once we eliminate the impossible...
WATSON	Whatever remains, however improbable, must be the truth.
HOLMES	Looked at that way it's rather obvious.
WATSON	Is it?
HOLMES	The person who smoked this cigar... got in here via a secret door.

A voice is heard from the darkness...

ADLER	Took you long enough.

...and Irene ADLER appears from the shadows.

Hello Sherlock Holmes.

HOLMES	Miss Adler.

A beat.

I always suspected there was more to you than a common adventuress.

ADLER	Common?
HOLMES	Run-of-the-mill. Ordinary.
ADLER	Thanks, that actually makes it worse.

HOLMES	I didn't take you for a cigar smoker.
ADLER	You didn't take me for anything at all.
WATSON	Where the devil did you come from?
ADLER	The Forbidden Door.
WATSON	I beg your pardon?
ADLER	Story goes, when George IV commissioned John Nash to rebuild the Little Theatre in 1820, he had him craft this charming nook below the stage so his Majesty could, ah, take some time away from his wife and spend it with his mistresses. Plural.
HOLMES	George IV had one mistress. Maria Fitzherbert.
ADLER	One that you know about. And yet he had seven keys made. One for every night of the week. Go figure.

ADLER produces a double-ended key.

	This end opens a concealed door about a hundred yards down the street; *this* end, after an extremely spidery passage, opens up the wall behind that cabinet. We found out about the place; won the keys at an auction of "curios."

HOLMES	And who's "We?" L'Assemblea dei Furfanti?
WATSON	Would anyone mind if I sat down?
ADLER	You had that picture two years and you're just figuring that out now?
HOLMES	You wrote in your letter that that photograph was intended for the King of Bohemia, not I.
ADLER	And yet I knew *you'd* end up with it somehow. Funny.
WATSON	I'll sit down.
ADLER	I shan't ask how you've been since you clearly have no interest in my wellbeing.
HOLMES	Should I?
ADLER	Shouldn't you? With all that's going on?
HOLMES	And what exactly is going on?
ADLER	*(To WATSON)* He *is* the smart one, right?
WATSON	*(Grinning)* I'm enjoying this.
HOLMES	What is this assembly of yours?
ADLER	You saying you can't tell me?

HOLMES   I'd say you were a union of international intelligence agents, pooling resources and working together to protect each other's own interests.

A beat.

ADLER   I take it back Sherlock; that was pretty good.

WATSON   You're a *spy?*

ADLER   It has been known.

WATSON   For America?

ADLER   Occasionally. Other countries sometimes. I've worked for your Empire too. We're freelancers, what d'you expect?

HOLMES   What's this? Your base of operations?

ADLER   Everyone needs a bolt-hole. Even your former King.

HOLMES   The name? Scoundrels' Assembly?

ADLER   Jan's idea. He was... kind of our leader? He figured, if we were going to use this place... actors coming and going, quirky costumes, masks... people won't even see us. And if anyone did ask, we'd say we were rehearsing a play. "The Scoundrels' Assembly."

WATSON   Did you know the caretaker here thinks you're all ghosts?

A beat.

ADLER   Some of us are, now.

HOLMES   Oberstein?

ADLER   He was the latest.

A beat.

I need your help. We're being picked off one by one. I've no idea why.

HOLMES   When did it start?

ADLER   About a year ago. Jan, who I... mentioned; Jan Rijnders, my – the... ah...

HOLMES   Rijnders. Dutch?

ADLER nods.

And your leader? Or your lover?

ADLER   Both. If you must know.

HOLMES   Have you always smoked his brand?

ADLER   Only when I'm here.

HOLMES   Continue.

ADLER	Jan was approached by a boy while walking near his home. Just an urchin, he said. Handed him a note. On it, his name, his aliases, current address in London... everything. Even details of his next assignment. Intelligence gathering in Persia on behalf of the Ottoman Empire.
WATSON	My word.
ADLER	Writer of the note knew of the Scoundrels' Assembly and had an offer.
HOLMES	Go on.
ADLER	He claimed to have a line on intelligence of the highest calibre, which we could have access to... if we would serve certain agendas. Specifically... his.
HOLMES	I see.
ADLER	We were given seven days to discuss it, and we were to post our response in the usual way.

HOLMES looks at ADLER, expecting more detail.

	Fake advertisements for the play. We adjusted the wording... to...
HOLMES	Leave messages for different clients.

ADLER nods.

	I take it this time your response was a "no."
ADLER	After we declined... we were told to look out for a "warning." Two days later Jan was captured on assignment, and... tortured to death in a Persian jail. We were going to marry.

Pause. ADLER is clearly upset.

HOLMES	If you would like the photograph returned...
ADLER	He's not in the picture. He took the picture. And he was just the first. Yevgeny was next. This guy right here. He was our Scaramuccia.
HOLMES	Yevgeny Kurzenov. A Russian. Also on Mycroft's list. Listed as "missing."
ADLER	He's not missing. He was killed in Madrid last September. Beaten so bad you could barely recognise him. Whole thing was staged to look like a street brawl. Next came... Pantalone. His real name was Adolphus.
HOLMES	Adolphus Meyer?

ADLER	*(Nods)* D'you read about the body discovered on the Chiltern Hills a couple weeks ago? No hands, no feet; face gnawed away by rats?
WATSON	I did. Police said it was more than likely an itinerant labourer.
ADLER	The Police didn't get the notes we did.
HOLMES	Notes?
ADLER	Arrived after each death.
HOLMES	Do you still have them?
ADLER	Louis has them.
HOLMES	LaRotière?
ADLER	You sure know a lot about us.
HOLMES	He's in London currently, I believe.
ADLER	I doubt it. He was jittery before Oberstein was killed; now he's straight up terrified. We all are. There's only three of us left. Louis, Eduardo and myself. And it doesn't seem to matter that we're clearly not a threat to... whoever's doing this...
HOLMES	...it's the fact that you know such a figure exists. Correct?
ADLER	That's my feeling, yeah.

HOLMES	The notes – you read them?

ADLER nods.

	Obscure quotes?
ADLER	That's right.
HOLMES	Signed with a single letter?
ADLER	No; unsigned. The single letter... that's new.
HOLMES	Thought as much. *(To WATSON)* The "M" was for us.
ADLER	You know who it is?

HOLMES nods.

	Who?
HOLMES	A very, very dangerous man. One I intend to stop at all costs. Until I do, I would advise you to stay undercover.

ADLER removes the double-ended key and hands it to HOLMES.

	What's this for?
ADLER	The seven people who had these... are, or were, family. You can call this a symbol of trust.

A beat.

I'll keep an eye on the press. In case the play gets advertised again. Don't worry. I have Jan's old key. I can get back here if I need to.

ADLER looks directly at HOLMES.

Find him, Sherlock. Hunt him down.

She exits.

WATSON That was... unexpected.

HOLMES To you, perhaps.

HOLMES has spotted something.

WATSON Come now, Holmes. Even if you *can* claim to have tracked these spies down, you can't have predicted that - *(Irene Adler would be here)*

HOLMES Someone else was in this room.

WATSON What?

HOLMES Before Miss Adler.

WATSON The caretaker?

HOLMES Smith? He wouldn't even come down the stairs. No, whoever they were accessed the room with a key like this one. They were tall and most likely male.

WATSON How do you know that?

HOLMES indicates a picture on the wall.

HOLMES   Because they moved that picture.
                      See the swept finger marks in the
                      dust on the edge of the frame?

WATSON   I... I do *now*, but...

HOLMES   The picture is approximately four
                      degrees off square, too. What does
                      that tell us?

WATSON   That it was removed?

HOLMES   More than that. The seven people
                      with access to this room would know
                      how to replace a picture so that no-
                      one would notice. I believe the
                      person who moved *this* picture
                      wanted the removal to be discovered.

WATSON   To what end?

HOLMES   So the discoverer would do likewise.

*Music. HOLMES removes a frame from the wall of
the set. Behind it, a clean patch of wallpaper frames a
card pinned to the plasterwork.*

Handkerchief, Watson.

*WATSON hands HOLMES a handkerchief. He
carefully removes the card, smells it, then breathes a
sigh of relief and gives the hankie back to WATSON.*

	(Reading) "Quand l'ennemi fait un faux mouvement, il faut se garder de l'interrompre. M."
WATSON	"When the enemy makes... a false... movement...?"
HOLMES	"When your enemy makes a mistake, it's important not to interrupt him." Napoleon.
WATSON	So... does that mean one of the surviving Scoundrels is working with Moriarty?
HOLMES	Or that he himself has the key of one of the dead ones. Either way, I don't think this quote was meant for Miss Adler to find.
WATSON	Us?
HOLMES	I'm afraid so. Let's close up here; get back to Baker Street.
WATSON	What mistake have we made?
A beat.	
	Getting involved in the first place, I suppose.
HOLMES	On the contrary. Now the game is afoot. For him as well as us.
WATSON	I don't understand. He was hidden.

HOLMES	He was waiting. There's a difference. And the closer we get, the more dangerous he'll become...

Music. The stage is reconfigured. We are back at Baker Street. MRS. HUDSON, DeWILDE and LESTRADE move the furniture and form a tableau for the arriving HOLMES and WATSON to join. HOLMES looks at the two visitors.

MRS. HUDSON	I'm sorry sir; they insisted.
HOLMES	It's all right Mrs. Hudson. Good evening Lestrade. Sir James.
WATSON	To what do we owe this pleasure?
LESTRADE	It's Mr. Holmes we've come to see.
WATSON	I'll leave you in peace.
HOLMES	Please, Watson; stay. I prefer to receive bad news in company.
DeWILDE	*(To HOLMES)* How do you know...?
HOLMES	Inspector Lestrade rubs his right hand over his left and shifts from foot to foot when preparing to deliver the worst.
LESTRADE	Do I?
MRS. HUDSON	You do.

A beat.

I know, I know. I'm going.

MRS. HUDSON exits. FITZMAURICE stands from HOLMES' chair.

DeWILDE   Mr. Holmes, Dr. Watson... allow me to introduce Henry Petty-Fitzmaurice. Secretary of State for War.

FITZMAURICE   Gentlemen.

WATSON   Your servant, sir.

HOLMES   My brother has spoken of you.

FITZMAURICE   His opinion of me is not unknown. Are you happy to speak in front of...

HOLMES nods.

                   Very well. *(To LESTRADE)* Proceed.

LESTRADE   Despite the lateness of the hour, I must advise you that I am here in my official capacity... and as such, anything you say may be taken down.

HOLMES   I am so advised.

DeWILDE   Have you had any contact with your brother at all?

HOLMES   My brother? Why?

LESTRADE looks at FITZMAURICE. He nods.

LESTRADE	We have reason to believe that Mycroft Holmes has taken flight.
HOLMES	Who's "we?"
LESTRADE	In possession of a number of documents...
FITZMAURICE	...which he intends to sell.
HOLMES	My brother. A traitor. It's preposterous.
FITZMAURICE	Nevertheless.
HOLMES	*(To LESTRADE)* My God, man! You were in this room *last week* – you and Sir James both – when Mycroft asked me to stop precisely this!
LESTRADE	I... am here... to...
FITZMAURICE	A communiqué was received from a certain foreign agent this morning implicating Mycroft Holmes in several acts of treasonous espionage, including the conspiracy to steal the Bruce-Partington plans. His part in the prevention of said deed appears, on this evidence, to have been a blind.
WATSON	I don't believe it. I just – I don't believe it.

DeWILDE	I don't either.
FITZMAURICE	*(To DeWILDE)* You forget yourself, sir!
DeWILDE	*(To FITZMAURICE)* I have to say this. *(To HOLMES)* Officially I *am* a part of this search, but I respect your brother and I owe him no less than to tell you – I think he's being framed.
FITZMAURICE	You will hold your tongue.
DeWILDE	The fact is, whether the government wants to admit it or not –
LESTRADE	Sir James!
DeWILDE	There *is* a leak in the high corridors of power. And whoever's responsible is also more than capable, not only of finding a scapegoat, but of having them silenced before they can prove their innocence.
Music.	
HOLMES	What are you saying?
DeWILDE	I'm afraid... I'm afraid a Black Order has been drawn up against your brother. And signed.
HOLMES	*(To FITZMAURICE)* By you?

DeWILDE	I'm sorry Sherlock.
WATSON	What's a Black Order?
FITZMAURICE	A Black Order states that in order to protect the Crown, the Empire and her interests...
HOLMES	Dear God.
FITZMAURICE	...the subject of that order is to be executed with extreme prejudice.
HOLMES	In other words Watson, my brother... is a dead man.

Music swells. Lights fade.

End of Act One.

Act Two. *Lights. The action picks up from where it left off.*
HOLMES sinks into a chair, head in hands.

WATSON   Holmes?

LESTRADE   Gentlemen, perhaps we should give Mr. Holmes a little time.

FITZMAURICE   Out of the question.

DeWILDE   Henry, please. *(To LESTRADE)* Inspector, would you mind stepping out for a moment? You too, Doctor.

LESTRADE   Oh; of course...

LESTRADE and WATSON exit, then DeWILDE approaches HOLMES.

DeWILDE   *(To HOLMES)* Sherlock, I know that you and your brother are not close in the traditional sense, so you may not fully realise how vital his position has become. Mycroft is nothing less than the British Empire's lynchpin. On countless occasions his word has instructed, guided – even *commanded* – the most powerful nation on earth.

FITZMAURICE   Whether one would want that or not.

HOLMES   *(To DeWILDE)* I am aware.

DeWILDE	The merest suspicion that these accusations have any basis in fact, you will lose a brother, I a mentor...
FITZMAURICE	Mentor. Dear Lord.
DeWILDE	...and the vacuum within government will be crippling. Put simply, there is a very real chance that England cannot function without Mycroft Holmes. *(Calling)* Inspector? Doctor?

LESTRADE and WATSON return.

FITZMAURICE	Now, I am prepared to seek a meeting with the Prime Minister to lift the Black Order, but that takes time. I should certainly like to prevent any embarrassment, however; so if you'd pay us the courtesy of letting us know where he is...

HOLMES appears as if he's just about holding himself together.

HOLMES	*(To LESTRADE)* You've checked his home and his club of course.
LESTRADE	His home's been ransacked. No-one's seen him at the Diogenes club.
HOLMES	Then I'm not sure how much help I can be. My brother is a creature of

near unbreakable habit. He has his rails and he runs on them. *(To DeWILDE)* What can you tell me about this communiqué?

DeWILDE looks at FITZMAURICE. He nods reluctantly.

DeWILDE   It follows protocol – tonally it's similar to previous correspondence with the agent... though the handwriting *does* get progressively unsteady.

HOLMES   Don't suppose I could see it, wherever it is?

LESTRADE   Mr. Holmes; now...

HOLMES nods.

HOLMES   *(To DeWILDE)* The agent, then. The one who wrote the letter.

DeWILDE   My hands are tied.

HOLMES   Understood.

DeWILDE   Outside of saying he was known to Mycroft.

HOLMES   Thank you. Thank you.

FITZMAURICE   *(To   DeWILDE)*   I   am   unaccustomed, sir...!

DeWILDE	He deserves to know a *little* more, surely.
FITZMAURICE	Deserves? May I remind you that *we* are the ones seeking information! Sparing no blushes, we have no idea how one brother's flight – genuine or otherwise – might have been aided by the other. Quite frankly Sir James, your conduct this evening is nothing less than a black mark on your character and your position. Good evening.

FITZMAURICE exits. A beat.

LESTRADE	We should... *(leave)*
DeWILDE	Of course. *(To HOLMES)* I'm so sorry about Fitzmaurice.
HOLMES	The apologies are mine to give. My manner has been... brusque, and...
DeWILDE	No offence taken. We're all on edge. If you think of anything. Anything at all. Anywhere he might be...
HOLMES	He's always spoken fondly of the Derbyshire Peaks. If you know them.

A beat.

DeWILDE	Vaguely.

HOLMES   Whatever you can do, Sir James. I'll be forever in your debt.

A beat. HOLMES appears to be quite emotional.

WATSON   Gentlemen, if you wouldn't mind...

DeWILDE   At once. Come, Inspector. Thank you, Doctor.

LESTRADE   All the best to you.

LESTRADE and DeWILDE exit. WATSON looks at HOLMES.

WATSON   Holmes, you so rarely discuss your brother, that – well, I had no idea you were quite this fond. I'll get Mrs. Hudson to make you a hot toddy before I leave. I'll be here first thing tomorrow, then we'll see what to do about Mycroft.

There is the sound of a horse and carriage departing under the tail end of this line. At once, HOLMES sits up. All upset has fallen from him, and he is absolutely fine.

HOLMES   Nothing.

WATSON   *(Surprised)* What?

HOLMES   Brother Mycroft's fine for now.

WATSON   What the devil?

HOLMES	Would you mind checking the window?
WATSON	Why?
HOLMES	We're being watched. Probably have been for a while.

WATSON heads downstage as if to the window. HOLMES starts to search the room for something – shelves, cabinets, drawers.

WATSON	From where?
HOLMES	A window, a balcony... street corner, perhaps. Most likely all three, in rotation.
WATSON	Who's watching us?

HOLMES looks at WATSON.

Moriarty?

HOLMES	Do you doubt it? This business with my brother is but a hint of his range. *(He resumes his search)* Oh, where the devil...?

WATSON turns away from the window.

WATSON	I can't see anything.

HOLMES sits in his chair but is up in an instant and clearly agitated.

Can you be sure Mycroft will be fine with this, this Black Order business?

HOLMES	I admit it is a *little* inconvenient, though he ought to be far enough away by now. *(Indicating WATSON's cane)* Do you mind?

WATSON knocks three times on the floor again.

WATSON	What do you mean, "far enough away?" Do you know where he is?
HOLMES	Beyond the reach of any Black Order.
WATSON	If you knew that, why did you pretend to be so upset?
HOLMES	Because if Moriarty's watching *us*, he's almost certainly watching our visitors too. Any conversation about my concerns over Mycroft must appear genuine.

MRS. HUDSON enters.

MRS. HUDSON	*(To HOLMES)* You thumped?
HOLMES	My brother's list of agents... you wouldn't happen to...
MRS. HUDSON	Already on my way.

She exits.

WATSON	Petty-Fitzmaurice was a... well, he was...

HOLMES	It's no secret there's no love lost between he and my brother.

WATSON	Would you like *me* to tell Lestrade or deWilde about Mycroft's whereabouts? Get a message to them in secret, or...?

HOLMES shakes his head.

HOLMES	Lestrade would be dutybound to report it. As for the "Senior Adviser..."

MRS. HUDSON enters holding the list MYCROFT gave to WATSON..

(To MRS. HUDSON) Ah! Perfect.

She hands the list to HOLMES, who scans it.

WATSON	What are you looking for?

HOLMES	DeWilde said that the communiqué which started this whole witch hunt was sent by a spy *known to Mycroft*. We know it's not Oberstein – we saw him killed... and we know from the Woman –

HOLMES sees WATSON and MRS. HUDSON looking at him.

...from *Miss Adler* – about the deaths of Rijnders, Kurzenov and Meyer. That leaves two names: Eduardo

Lucas of Godolphin Street, Westminster, and Louis LaRotière – Campden Mansions, Notting Hill. And since Eduardo Lucas was last seen in Paris...

HOLMES turns to MRS. HUDSON.

(To MRS. HUDSON) Mr. & Mrs. Aspinall will be taking a trip to Notting Hill.

MRS. HUDSON   Now?

HOLMES   They will.

MRS. HUDSON   Give me five minutes.

Flashing a quick smile at WATSON, MRS. HUDSON exits. HOLMES pulls a trunk from under a table and removes from it a wig of some description.

WATSON   So... as well as feigning upset, you also *feigned* warming to Sir James?

HOLMES   As long as he feels like I'm in his debt, he won't push for more and we'll have him off our backs.

He pulls on the wig.

WATSON   You tipped him off as to Mycroft's whereabouts.

HOLMES   Did I?

WATSON   Your mention of Derbyshire...

HOLMES continues to dress, putting on and tying a tatty old scarf &c.

HOLMES My brother knows no more about the Peak District than I do the back end of the moon. I do hope it gives our "Senior Advisor" something to think about, however.

He changes his coat for something far less well tailored.

Do you recall *our* trip up to the Peaks? Some years ago now...

WATSON The Priory School kidnapping?

HOLMES Indeed.

WATSON One of the first cases you invited me on. The Duke's bastard son, with the heterochromia. One green eye, one brown.

HOLMES That's the one. Might be worth revisiting that at some point...

HOLMES turns to WATSON.

How do I look?

WATSON Ghastly.

HOLMES Hoped as much. *(Calling off)* Are you ready?

MRS. HUDSON *(Off)* Will be if you stop rushing me.

WATSON   What is all this?

HOLMES   This, my dear Watson, is me saying goodnight. Go and spend the evening with Mary. There's work to be done in Notting Hill.

WATSON   Then shouldn't we – *(head over there together)*

HOLMES   Not this time. Anyone watching the house cannot see the pair of us exiting together. No, we shall leave this business to the Aspinalls.

WATSON   Who are the Aspinalls?

MRS. HUDSON enters, also in a very convincing disguise.

BOTH   *(Together; Cockney accent)* We are.

Music. HOLMES and MRS. HUDSON exit. WATSON moves downstage. He places two whisky tumblers on a table or crate, then proceeds to lay chairs on their sides, scatter papers about and make the space appear broken into as he speaks.

WATSON   *(To audience)* At some point following my return to civil practice, Holmes had recruited our housekeeper to share certain assignments with him – his remarkable skill with disguises having been passed on, to an extent.

They had even gone so far as to register 221A Baker Street – long empty – as the residence of "the Aspinalls," so on those occasions when Holmes felt eyes upon him and needed to exit incognito, he and Mrs. Hudson could leave Baker Street in the guise of a couple. So it was that at close to eleven o'clock that Tuesday night, "the Aspinalls" reached the Notting Hill residence of Louis LaRotière to find the door unlocked and open...

WATSON moves to the side of the stage and watches as HOLMES and MRS. HUDSON enter and look around them. HOLMES holds a lantern.

MRS. HUDSON   Someone beat us to it.

HOLMES   So I see...

He draws a revolver from his belt. Music. They move into the room.

MRS. HUDSON   Oh Lord... what happened in here?

HOLMES   Nothing good.

He moves to the table. Smells one of the glasses.

Lagavulin. A fine single malt.

HOLMES hands MRS. HUDSON the lantern.

	Take this, Mrs. Aspinall.
MRS. HUDSON	Where are you going?
HOLMES	There's a light in the bedroom. I'll check in there.
MRS. HUDSON	What do I do?
HOLMES	Stay in here. And don't touch anything.

He exits. MRS. HUDSON whispers after him.

| **MRS. HUDSON** | I wasn't planning to! |

As MRS. HUDSON approaches the other doorway an arm suddenly flops into view. The hand is streaked with blood. MRS. HUDSON shrieks. There is a voice from off; that of a NEIGHBOUR.

| **NEIGHBOUR** | *(Off)* Bloody hell! Keep it down in there! |

HOLMES returns with a second lantern and sees it.

| **HOLMES** | Monsieur LaRotière, I presume. |
| **MRS. HUDSON** | I think he's... I think... |

HOLMES pulls a bloody letter opener from the victim. He brings it to the lantern.

	God save us.
HOLMES	Buried in his neck.
MRS. HUDSON	A knife?

| HOLMES | Letter opener. And unless I'm much mistaken it's my brother's. |

| MRS. HUDSON | I'm going to be sick. I think I'm going to be sick... |

MRS. HUDSON turns away. HOLMES takes out a handkerchief and cleans the blade.

Your brother wouldn't...?

| HOLMES | No. But we're meant to think he did. |

HOLMES wraps the weapon in the hankie and puts it in his pocket.

Right, let's have a look at you...

He bends over and inspects the body.

| MRS. HUDSON | Careful... |

| HOLMES | There's nothing to be scared of Mrs. Hudson; this man is – *(dead)* |

As HOLMES moves the body slightly, LaROTIÈRE lets out a final groan which takes even HOLMES by surprise. MRS. HUDSON screams again and they both stand up.

| NEIGHBOUR | *(Off)* Keep the bloody noise down! Last warning! |

A moment of stillness. HOLMES and MRS. HUDSON wait. HOLMES crouches again; feels for a pulse.

| MRS. HUDSON | He's still alive! |

HOLMES	No.
MRS. HUDSON	He made a noise!
HOLMES	Air escaping the lungs, nothing more. Now...

HOLMES returns to his inspection.

> Badly beaten... deep cut in neck... three fingers on right hand broken – those injuries at least a day old... rope marks and scratches around left wrist. He's been bound, then cut himself free.

HOLMES spots the blood-smeared sheet of paper in LAROTIÈRE's hand.

> Hello...

He retrieves it.

MRS. HUDSON	What's it say?
HOLMES	*(Reading)* "The pen is mightier than the sword."
MRS. HUDSON	Funny last words.
HOLMES	Not his.

HOLMES stands.

> Mrs. Hudson, if you can bear it, see if you can find where Monsieur LaRotière was tied up.

MRS. HUDSON   If it means not looking at him, I can
                     bear it.

> *MRS. HUDSON passes the body and exits.*
> *HOLMES sniffs the paper he's holding.*

                     (Off) Ohhhhhh... there's so much
                     blood...

HOLMES   *(Calling off)* I don't doubt that.

> *HOLMES looks at the hand.*

MRS. HUDSON   *(Off)* Found it!

> *He sniffs LaROTIÈRE's fingers. Realises something.*
> *MRS. HUDSON enters.*

                     He must have been tied to the pantry
                     door. Cut his way through the rope –

HOLMES   By smashing a jar of vinegar.

MRS. HUDSON   How'd you know that?

> *HOLMES holds up the paper.*

HOLMES   Hold the lantern here, would you?

> *HOLMES positions MRS. HUDSON's arms so the*
> *lantern is behind the paper, then brings it very close*
> *to the flame within.*

MRS. HUDSON   Any closer and you'll set it on fire.

HOLMES   Steady...

MRS. HUDSON   What are you doing?

After a moment he holds the paper out to her.

HOLMES   Vinegar is a natural invisible ink. I have a feeling our friend here had one last trick up his sleeve. See? LaRotière's *actual* message. *(Reading)* "Sous l'armoire."

MRS. HUDSON   Who's this Sue now?

HOLMES   It's French. It means "Under the wardrobe."

MRS. HUDSON   What is?

HOLMES   Something worth killing for...

HOLMES moves to the exit again, then turns.

Come on Mrs. Aspinall.

Music. They exit. WATSON stands and straightens up the space as he narrates.

WATSON   *(To audience)* The incidents of the previous night were related to me the following morning at Baker Street. Holmes was in high spirits despite only having had, according to him, a few minutes repose on the chaise longue. This was his way – come the end of the affair he'd be fit for nothing, but for now? Boundless energy...

HOLMES enters holding a red file.

HOLMES	Attached to the underside of the wardrobe, would you believe? Almost missed it at first, then Mrs. Hudson moved the lantern and the shifting shadow revealed all...

HOLMES hands the red file to WATSON.

WATSON	What is it?
HOLMES	Notes for a report on government leaks. Commissioned by my brother.
WATSON	And stolen by LaRotière?
HOLMES	Prepared by him.

A beat.

WATSON	Mycroft was *working* with LaRotière?

HOLMES nods. MRS. HUDSON enters with a newspaper.

MRS. HUDSON	Paper.
WATSON	I'm sorry; this chap prepares a report for your brother... then writes a damning communiqué about him?
MRS. HUDSON	Put it over here, shall I?
HOLMES	That communiqué was not LaRotière's idea.
WATSON	Oh?

HOLMES	He was coerced into writing it.
MRS. HUDSON	Had his fingers broken. *(To HOLMES)* Didn't he?
HOLMES	Hence the worsening handwriting deWilde mentioned.
WATSON	When?
HOLMES	Let us create a timeline; it may serve us. At some point before yesterday morning, LaRotière was visited by someone he knew – someone he was pleased to see, even. They drink some rather expensive whisky together; All seems well... but then the visitor wants something.
WATSON	The file.
HOLMES	LaRotière is overpowered. To buy himself time, LaRotière tells whoever's there that the file has already been handed over.
WATSON	To Mycroft.
HOLMES	Our visitor then forces LaRotière to write his communiqué, implicating my brother in all manner of treasonous activity. The Frenchman is tied to the pantry door while the visitor heads to Pall Mall.
MRS. HUDSON	Ransacks your brother's place.

HOLMES	Once he realises he's been lied to, he takes the letter opener, returns to Notting Hill, beats LaRotière still further... stabs him in the neck...
MRS. HUDSON	Don't. Please.
HOLMES	...and tears *his* place apart as well.
WATSON	But leaves empty-handed?
MRS. HUDSON	Disturbed by the neighbours most likely.
HOLMES	Whereupon LaRotière, mortally wounded, but now freed from his bonds by the smashed vinegar jar, makes it to the kitchen and writes a note for Mycroft, tipping him off to the location of this red file before succumbing.

WATSON starts to look through it.

WATSON	Let's see... newspaper adverts for "The Scoundrels' Assembly..."
MRS. HUDSON	Told you I'd seen it advertised.
WATSON	Didn't Miss Adler said they used these...
HOLMES	...to keep in touch with their contacts. See at the top of that one there.

WATSON and MRS. HUDSON look at a newspaper clipping.

WATSON   *(Reading)* "Being for the benefit of M. Croft."

MRS. HUDSON   Bless me. Mycroft.

WATSON   *(Reading)* "Tickets now on sale?"

HOLMES   I would take that to mean, "Work has commenced."

WATSON   Remarkable.

HOLMES   Several others declare, "Tickets *still* on sale."

MRS. HUDSON   Most of 'em by the looks.

WATSON   "Work still in progress?"

HOLMES   Or words to that effect. Now look at this.

HOLMES slides a sheet of paper across to WATSON.

                     I believe *that* would have been in today's paper, had LaRotière not been intercepted and killed.

WATSON   *(Reading)* "All tickets sold. Exclusive run opens Sunday. Little Theatre Beneath."

HOLMES   The report's finished. Collect it on Sunday.

WATSON   Is it in there?

HOLMES pulls something else out of the file and hands it to WATSON.

                    What's this?

HOLMES   The report.

WATSON   In code?

HOLMES   Alas. Tonal as a base, but with variations.

MRS. HUDSON   Shouldn't there be a key?

HOLMES   I suspect the key was in LaRotière's head.

MRS. HUDSON   Making this here file useless?

HOLMES   It's not unsolvable. Besides, there are other things of use in here...

HOLMES brings out a few handwritten notes.

WATSON   Are those are the notes Moriarty sent to the Scoundrels?

MRS. HUDSON   Notes?

HOLMES   The Professor sent them after each one was killed. Quotes, all of them. First, the one sent from Persia after Rijnders' demise. March last year.

He hands the clipping to WATSON.

WATSON	*(Reading)* "Peace in international relations is a period of cheating between two periods of fighting." *(Puzzled)* Miss Adler said this Rijnders fellow was spying for the Ottoman Empire. Persia and the Ottomans aren't at odds.
HOLMES	No indeed. Next, this one. Posted in Madrid six months later, following the death of Yevgeny Kurzenov.

WATSON takes the next note from HOLMES.

WATSON	*(Reading)* "The more corrupt the state, the more numerous the laws."
HOLMES	Roman Emperor Tacitus.

WATSON takes another.

WATSON	*(Reading)* "The true measure of a man is what he would do if he knew he would never be caught."
HOLMES	That one arrived after Adolphus Meyer's dismembered corpse was found on the Chilterns. That was just a few weeks ago. January.
WATSON	*(Turning it over)* "Never be caught... never..."
HOLMES	Chronologically, we then have the Oberstein card about the innocent... and if we assume the note in the

118

	theatre was meant specifically for *us*, that brings us to this one.
WATSON	"The pen is mightier than the sword."
HOLMES	Left with the body as opposed to having been posted.
WATSON	No-one left to collect it.
MRS. HUDSON	Then why leave it at all?
HOLMES	For me. It's not good enough that he can beat me – he wants me to *know* that he can.
WATSON	He hasn't beaten you!
HOLMES	My brother's in mortal danger and several people are dead. If there's an upper hand in this exchange, the Professor has it.
WATSON	In the one quantifiable way, the Bruce-Partington Affair, you came out on top. The rest is bluster; just things that have already happened.
Music.	
HOLMES	My God. My God, you've got it!

In an instant HOLMES is rifling through the red file – notes, clippings and all – speaking in an excited manner.

Communicating that you've done something after the fact - you're right, it's braggadocio, nothing more... but... *but...*

MRS. HUDSON   But what?

HOLMES holds up a note.

HOLMES   This one. Here. The quote posted after Meyer's death. "The true measure of a man is what he would do if he knew he would never be caught."

WATSON   Yes?

HOLMES   Meyer's body was found last month. Two weeks later, on the night we apprehended Colonel Walter, it's what *he* said to *us!* Almost word for word, I swear it!

He holds up another note.

And this! The Tacitus quote – posted *after* Kurzenov was killed in Madrid last September. "The more corrupt the state, the more numerous the laws." Watson, you follow politics. Do you consider Spain to be particularly corrupt?

WATSON   Disorganised more than corrupt, I'd say.

HOLMES	Quite. But... remember the chap dismissed from the War Office on charges of corruption... you mentioned him not so long ago...
WATSON	Thomas Beattie?
HOLMES	The very man. Exposed in October, correct? Early October?
WATSON	Sounds about right.
HOLMES	A matter of weeks *after* Kurzenov's death, but long enough *before* Beattie was disgraced!
WATSON	I suppose...
HOLMES	There's no suppose about it. These quotes don't reflect the murders that preceded them. *That's* how he's taunting us! Oh, you are clever, Professor. He's offering us a glimpse of what he's *going* to do, assuming that by the time we figure it out, he will have done it.
MRS. HUDSON	I don't follow.
WATSON	I'm not sure I do either.
HOLMES	Each Scoundrel's death has been followed by a quote, correct?
WATSON	Yes.
HOLMES	And each quote precedes a crime...

121

WATSON   Well, we don't know that yet.

HOLMES   It's what we have so far. Quote, crime. Quote, crime. Or, in Beattie's case, the exposure of one.

WATSON   Moriarty had a hand in the downfall of Thomas Beattie?

HOLMES   Certainly. Doubtless the murders of the Scoundrels serve a purpose all their own, but if we regard them as red herrings and remove them, we are left with a second agenda. One that the Professor has planned to the letter.

MRS. HUDSON   What is it?

HOLMES   There are not enough data as yet. We shall follow the quotes. They're the key.

WATSON   Where do we start?

HOLMES   With the most recent.

MRS. HUDSON   "The pen is mightier than the sword?"

WATSON looks at MRS. HUDSON.

                         I do pay attention.

HOLMES   Watson, check the newspapers. Look for stories about laws, letters, documents... anything that could

	bring shame – or worse – on the government.
WATSON	Would that sort of thing be in the paper?
HOLMES	We can but hope. *(To MRS. HUDSON)* Mrs. Hudson, I wonder if you wouldn't mind helping fill in some of the gaps?
MRS. HUDSON	How do I do that?
HOLMES	Start with the Oberstein quote. "The innocent seldom find an uneasy pillow." Look for unexplained deaths of innocent citizens in the last fortnight.
MRS. HUDSON	Then what?
HOLMES	Then it's the Rijnders quote, so you'd be looking for anything to do with peace, international relations... for that you'll need to go to the Morgue.
MRS. HUDSON	I can't look at another dead body.
HOLMES	My dear Mrs. Hudson, the Morgue is the name given to the *Times* newspaper archive. Have a look back to anything in a three-month range. That should cover it. Start in March last year.

MRS. HUDSON	Three *months?* Might take a while.
HOLMES	There's a chap there; name of Fennell. Give him my name; he'll help you find what you need. If you're willing.
MRS. HUDSON	I am not.

A beat.

(Grinning) But Mrs. Aspinall might be.

Music. The stage is reconfigured. HOLMES and MRS. HUDSON exit.

WATSON
(To audience) The next few days were an agony of waiting. I checked every newspaper I could get my hands on for any hint of Moriarty's plans, but in vain. Holmes stalked the rooms of Baker Street, growing increasingly frustrated – he always swore off cocaine whilst engaged with a problem, and since he had no chemicals to experiment with, it meant only one thing:

There is the atonal scraping of a violin. MRS. HUDSON enters with a newspaper.

At least Mrs. Hudson was making progress with Mr. Fennell at the Morgue...

She slaps down the paper in front of WATSON.

MRS. HUDSON   Alma Waters.

WATSON   Who?

MRS. HUDSON   Artist; one of the first women tutors at Bedford College. Killed in her bed last week. Smothered... by a pillow.

WATSON   "The innocent seldom find an uneasy pillow..."

MRS. HUDSON   She's the innocent.

Another unpleasant violin note.

WATSON   Do the police have a suspect?

MRS. HUDSON   Several. Apparently since the passing of her husband she'd been taking in lodgers – undesirables, mostly – using them as subjects of her art in lieu of rent. Current suspicion points to one of those, though according to this they all thought of her as an "angel."

WATSON   What's Alma Waters got to do with any of this?

MRS. HUDSON   That's a question for the maestro, not me.

Another violin note.

I'm off to the archive. Herbert's waiting for me.

WATSON Herbert, is it?

MRS. HUDSON We've been going through the papers together. That's all.

MRS. HUDSON picks up a tin. WATSON spots it.

And we might have been sharing a bit of bun-loaf.

WATSON raises a knowing eyebrow.

What? Nice to meet someone who appreciates my baking.

She exits.

WATSON *(To audience)* After a week with no hint of Moriarty's intentions I went back to my practice, not returning to Baker Street for eight perfectly ordinary days. When I did, summoned on a rain-soaked, grim-grey Wednesday by one of Holmes' urchins, I arrived to find a nervous looking woman pacing the parlour, while in the study...

DeWILDE enters from an internal room within Baker Street. WATSON turns into the scene. Lights.

DeWILDE Good morning, Watson.

WATSON Sir James...

DeWILDE	Fascinating room.
WATSON	Yes, it's... where Holmes conducts his experiments. Sorry, where is he?
DeWILDE	Consulting with one of my colleagues. He'll be along directly.
WATSON	I take it your superior doesn't know you're here?
DeWILDE	No. After our last visit I thought it wiser... we're here by order of the Prime Minister himself.
WATSON	Oh...?

HOLMES enters, followed by TREL-HOPE.

HOLMES	Ah! There you are. Watson, this is Alexander Trelawney-Hope.
TREL-HOPE	Yes, I'm the, er...
WATSON	The Minister for European Affairs.
DeWILDE	*(To TREL-HOPE)* Told you he followed politics.
WATSON	*(To HOLMES)* There's a woman in the parlour...
TREL-HOPE	My wife. She knows nothing of our purpose here.
TREL-HOPE	I happened to mention I was going to see Sherlock Holmes, and... she's

something of a fan. Of your books, Doctor.

WATSON   *(Pleased)* Well...

HOLMES   *(To TREL-HOPE)* Mr. Trelawney-Hope, to return to the purpose you spoke of... would you mind recapping?

TREL-HOPE   No, no. *(To WATSON)* I apologise for my manner – I'm in something of a mess. Ah... put simply, a rather important document was stolen from a locked dispatch box in my bedroom last night.

WATSON   From...?

HOLMES   Yes. Between seven-thirty and eleven-thirty would be my estimation.

TREL-HOPE   How, how, how did you... *(narrow it down?)*

HOLMES   You mentioned that you and your wife left your home at Whitehall Terrace at seven-thirty – you to dine, your wife to attend the theatre. You yourself arrived home a little after ten but you waited up for the return of your wife at eleven, the both of you retiring to bed at half past.

TREL-HOPE	That's correct.
HOLMES	You further mentioned that you are both light sleepers, thus significantly reducing the possibility of a break-in after that point.
WATSON	The Police have been informed, I take it.
DeWILDE	To inform the Police is to inform the public. We're avoiding that.
WATSON	Because...?
TREL-HOPE	The consequences of this document's publication would be dire.
DeWILDE	Unless its recovery can be attended with the utmost secrecy, the end result would almost certainly be war.

WATSON and HOLMES share a look.

HOLMES	"The pen is mightier than the sword."
WATSON	*(To TREL-HOPE)* Could anyone among your staff have known that there was something extraordinary in the dispatch box?
TREL-HOPE	I don't see how.
WATSON	Surely your wife knew.

TREL-HOPE	No, sir. I never discuss politics with my wife. In fact I said nothing to her until I let slip that I was coming here.
HOLMES	This document... a letter, correct?

TREL-HOPE nods.

	Received?
TREL-HOPE	Six days ago.
WATSON	Who knows of its existence?
TREL-HOPE	The Cabinet were informed last week.

TREL-HOPE nods towards DeWILDE.

	Along with one or two... departmental officials.
HOLMES	And what does the letter contain?
TREL-HOPE	The fewer people that know of its content the better.
HOLMES	I must know what is at stake. There is no other way forward.
DeWILDE	*(To TREL-HOPE)* We can trust them.

TREL-HOPE turns to HOLMES.

TREL-HOPE	It was sent by... a certain foreign leader, who has been ruffled by some

	of the Empire's recent Colonial developments...
DeWILDE	Secretary Fitzmaurice is proving to be... how to put this? Somewhat less than effective in the current campaign. After "Bloody Sunday" the Prime Minister approached Lord Kitchener to turn the tide of the war.
TREL-HOPE	His proposals are controversial.
WATSON	Such as?
DeWILDE	He means to employ a military destruction policy. Starving the Boer supply lines by burning farms and crops. Strategic devastation.
HOLMES	Aren't there indigenous peoples on those lands as well as Boers?
DeWILDE	There are.
WATSON	Good God...
TREL-HOPE	There's more.

TREL-HOPE looks at DeWILDE. He nods.

	Kitchener intends to build concentration camps. For Boer families. Wives. Children. And another camp for the Africans.

DeWILDE	It's a system of "isolation and attrition." All approved by the Prime Minister. And her Majesty.
TREL-HOPE	It appears however, in the early stages of these discussions, that a number of these proposals have managed to make their way across Europe.
HOLMES	The fuel for the letter.
WATSON	Do you think this leader might *want* it made public?
TREL-HOPE	No, we understand that he realises he has acted rashly. It would be a greater blow to *his* country were the letter to come out.
HOLMES	In that case, why should anyone desire to steal or publish it?
DeWILDE	Queen Victoria is ageing. Her heir sees European stability as vital. If we are drawn into a war in Europe – at the same time as our continuing campaign against the Boers – we risk that stability, could end up fighting lost causes on two fronts and the Empire as we know it will start to fragment. That *cannot* be her Majesty's legacy.
WATSON	Do you think that likely?

| DeWILDE | What you must understand is, the whole of Europe is an armed camp. There is a double league which makes a fair balance of military power. Great Britain holds the scales. If we were driven into war with one confederacy, it would assure the supremacy of the other. Do you follow? |
| HOLMES | It is in the interest of the *enemies* of this leader to secure and publish the letter, so as to create a breach between his country and ours. Correct? |

DeWILDE nods.

	Very well. I shall look into the matter.
DeWILDE	Thank you, Sherlock. Thank you.
TREL-HOPE	I'll send my wife up, if that's... *(all right)*
HOLMES	By all means.
TREL-HOPE	One last thing – we are to brief the Prime Minister this afternoon. What do we say?
HOLMES	You believe that unless this document is recovered there will be a second war?

DeWILDE	Most probably.
HOLMES	Tell him to prepare for war.

TREL-HOPE and DeWILDE exit.

The Professor's plans are revealed.

WATSON	You think Moriarty wants to see the British Empire fall?
HOLMES	Not quite, but I imagine he'd enjoy being the master of her fate. You heard Sir James – "Great Britain holds the scales?" I could think of nothing he'd prize more highly. Besides, keeping Britain in a perpetual state of war is extremely profitable for some.
WATSON	To manage that he'd have to emerge from the shadows, surely.
HOLMES	Not if the leak at the top of the chain is Moriarty's pawn.
WATSON	Fitzmaurice?
HOLMES	I shall make enquiries. Send telegrams to Moriarty's seats – Stonyhurst, Durham – see if Fitzmaurice attended either. If there's a connection we'll find it.

HILDA enters.

HILDA	I don't mean to intrude...

HOLMES	Mrs. Hope. Not at all.
HILDA	Mr. Holmes. It's an honour. *(To WATSON)* And Dr. Watson. I've read every account of your cases. *His* cases. Magnificent.
WATSON	Too kind.
HILDA	I take it Alexander came to ask you about the disturbance at our home?
HOLMES	He did.
HILDA	Then doubtless I'll be reading about it soon.

HILDA's smile falters and her head drops.

WATSON	Mrs. Trelawney-Hope?
HILDA	I'm sorry. I just... my husband never speaks about certain matters with me, but he told me something has been taken, and I... I know it must be serious...
WATSON	Come, madam...

WATSON hands HILDA a handkerchief.

HILDA	What will it lead to? Is his political career likely to suffer?
HOLMES	Better you ask him. It's really not my place.

HILDA dabs at her eyes with the handkerchief.

135

HILDA   Of course. Of course. I should never have gone out. None of this would have happened, if...

WATSON   That's no way to think. If you'd been at home, something far worse might have transpired. Holmes and I will do our best to recover it.

HILDA   Thank you both.

HILDA heads to the exit.

HOLMES   What did you see?

HILDA   I'm sorry?

HOLMES   At the theatre. What play did you take in?

A beat.

HILDA   Oh, it... it was called... "The Scoundrels' Assembly."

Music.

                    Have you seen it?

HOLMES   No, the... price of admission is too high.

HILDA and HOLMES lock eyes for a moment. Then:

HILDA   Good-day, gentlemen.

She exits. WATSON looks at HOLMES.

WATSON   I don't understand.

HOLMES holds his hand up to still WATSON.
Listens for a door shutting.

HOLMES   Allow me to explain. It appears Mrs. Trelawney-Hope was being blackmailed over something in her past – the exposure of a former lover most likely. The blackmailer – one of the remaining scoundrels, naturally – requested an exchange last night. The letter in her husband's dispatch box for... well. Whatever evidence Mrs. Hope wanted rid of.

WATSON   How the devil could you know that?

HOLMES   The flushing of her cheek, the touching of her wedding band, her general demeanour – the ink stains on her fingers, the tremor in her voice... there are several factors.

WATSON   So she *herself* stole the letter?

HOLMES   As plainly as she sat before us just now. How the Scoundrel got a hold of the leverage is one of only two remaining mysteries in this affair.

WATSON   The other being...?

HOLMES   Which Scoundrel it was. Watson, you head to Godolphin Street –

	Eduardo Lucas' place of residence. If he still has the letter, buy it.
WATSON	Are you serious?
HOLMES	Indeed I am. We have the coffers of the British government at our service.
WATSON	Where shall you go?
HOLMES	Back to that forbidden room beneath the theatre. If the Woman is there, and if she has the letter, I shall tell her that she has stolen it for the very man behind the deaths of her comrades. Hurry, Watson! The longer that letter is unaccounted for, the closer the country is to disaster...

Music. The stage is reconfigured.

| **WATSON** | *(To audience)* So while Holmes headed for the Little Theatre, I made for Godolphin Street, home of Eduardo Lucas... to be greeted by a familiar face which could only bode ill... |

LESTRADE enters.

LESTRADE	Doctor.
WATSON	Inspector.
LESTRADE	What are you doing here?

WATSON	Oh... Holmes...
LESTRADE	Don't tell me. I probably don't want to know. He not with you?
WATSON	Engaged on another matter.
LESTRADE	Don't tell me that either.
WATSON	I take it Mr. Lucas...
LESTRADE	Know his name, do you?

WATSON nods.

Course you do. Up there.

Music. WATSON climbs the stairs and opens the door at the top. WATSON recoils.

WATSON	Bloody hell.
LESTRADE	Literally.
WATSON	When did...?
LESTRADE	Last night, maybe around ten?

LESTRADE checks his notebook.

From half past nine, neighbours say they heard raised voices. Arguing escalated into what sounded like furniture being thrown – and, finally, screaming. Wasn't reported until this morning, though.

WATSON	Why not?

LESTRADE	If I knew that, I'd be the head of Scotland Yard by this time next year.
WATSON	The dagger?
LESTRADE	One of those fancy Arabian ones. He's got a load on the wall in a room back there. Funny thing... that room isn't disturbed at all. Seems the killer went specifically to that room for the blade, like he knew where to find it.
WATSON	Might I... we're looking for something the victim might have had in his possession...
LESTRADE	I can give you five minutes. No longer. I really shouldn't, but – after what Mr. Holmes went through the other night...
WATSON	Thank you, Inspector.

LESTRADE exits.

(To audience) The room was a butchers yard; blood soaking the rug and staining the boards beneath Lucas' stricken body. The dagger's curved blade had been thrust into his heart with some force – barely an inch of the sharpened steel remained outside the dead man's flesh. The victim's eyes distended in horror, his fists closed...but he held nothing. I

could find no trace of the letter in fact. I bid Lestrade good day and left the scene, intending to consult with Holmes... but on the corner of Godolphin Street...

HILDA enters.

HILDA

I didn't kill him.

WATSON

Mrs. Hope.

HILDA

I know he knows what Lucas had over me. Mr. Holmes, I mean. I've read too many of your accounts to fool myself.

WATSON dispatch box.

You took it from your husband's

HILDA

I didn't know what it was! That man, that *Lucas*, said it was a foreign matter, and of little consequence. He knew about my past! He knew everything! He had... letters I'd written. He offered them back to me... if... you know.

WATSON

Lucas arranged the trade?

HILDA

I was to say I was attending the theatre – but to come here instead. He gave me a fake ticket and everything. I made the exchange. Halfway home, I... changed my mind and returned, but... I heard such violence from within that I dared not knock again.

WATSON   And you're here now to recover the letter?

HILDA   Am I too late?

WATSON   We both are.

HILDA's head drops.

Madam, let me assure you, whatever was in your past is of no concern to Sherlock Holmes – his focus will remain solely on the return of that letter to the dispatch box.

HILDA   And my husband need never know?

WATSON   Of course not.

HILDA   Bless you, Dr. Watson. Bless you both.

HILDA exits. WATSON turns to the audience.

WATSON   *(To audience)* I watched the relieved figure of Mrs. Hope swallowed by the tide of London's busy streets and sought out a hansom to the Little Theatre. Holmes had been right on all counts. Scant comfort if the letter continued to elude us...

WATSON exits. Music. The stage is reconfigured. HOLMES enters, standing still in the space and looking rather preoccupied. WATSON enters.

(To HOLMES) Bad news on the letter front I'm afraid, though you were, as ever, completely correct as to Mrs... Hope...

WATSON stops.

Are you all right?

HOLMES   *He* was here.

WATSON   "He," as in...?

HOLMES   Moriarty. We spoke.

WATSON   What? When?

HOLMES   Less than an hour ago. He must have followed me down the passage.

WATSON   My God. What did he say to you?

Lights. MORIARTY enters. WATSON watches.

MORIARTY   Unusual place.

HOLMES freezes.

I take it you know its history. Might I sit?

HOLMES gestures to a seat. MORIARTY sits.

Your Doctor friend not here?

HOLMES looks at MORIARTY.

Pity. I should like to have at least made his acquaintance.

A beat.

And your housekeeper. Enjoying her time at the archive?

HOLMES What of it?

MORIARTY Hate for it to get her into trouble.

He reaches into his jacket and removes a notebook.

Now... in the last month your movements have inconvenienced me, your enquiries forced my hand, and now you and I, we stand at a crossroads.

HOLMES Is that so?

MORIARTY smiles.

MORIARTY It's always been an intellectual treat for me, seeing you grapple with a problem. It'd be a grief to have to take extreme measures with you.

HOLMES You already tried that, in the hotel.

MORIARTY If I thought you'd have actually fallen for that contact poison you wouldn't be worthy of this attention.

HOLMES I'm flattered.

MORIARTY	Such games as we have played in the past are easily brushed aside, as one might crumbs from a banquet table. My present engagements however, are altogether too delicious – and so I must ask you to withdraw. All of you.
HOLMES	Then why invite me in the first place?
MORIARTY	I didn't invite you; merely controlled your entry. I knew you'd come.
HOLMES	I cannot back down.
MORIARTY	You court danger otherwise.
HOLMES	Part of my trade.
MORIARTY	Your doctor friend's too? How about the housekeeper? And your brother? How's he getting on, wherever he is?

HOLMES says nothing.

	You're similar, you and him. Of course, his adherence to the status quo is a missed opportunity. You see that, don't you?
HOLMES	My brother knows his place.
MORIARTY	But not his position. His influence over government, over policy... it is

no less than a harness on the truth. And the person holding those reins can shape worlds.

HOLMES   If all this has been about Mycroft, why did the Scoundrels have to die?

MORIARTY   That you're even asking that shows how unprepared you are for what's to come.

HOLMES   "The pen is mightier than the sword?"

MORIARTY stands.

MORIARTY   The gears turn on that game even as we speak. Its aims are true. I've worked too hard to see them derailed.

MORIARTY turns to face HOLMES.

Stand clear. Or be trodden underfoot.

HOLMES nods, yet remains impassive. MORIARTY shakes his head. Smiles.

Look, you can't say I didn't try. I don't imagine we'll be seeing each other again.

HOLMES   Only if you persist.

MORIARTY takes a step towards HOLMES.

MORIARTY	Try to bring destruction upon me and I promise I shall do at least as much to you.
HOLMES	If I were assured of the former eventuality I would accept the latter.
MORIARTY	I'll bear that in mind...

MORIARTY exits. Lights.

WATSON	Do you think he meant it? All the threats?
HOLMES	Without question. Come, Watson. Let's return to Baker Street. Until we've turned this game in our favour, we're all at risk. Especially brother Mycroft, it seems.
WATSON	I thought he was safe.
HOLMES	A fortnight ago yes, but he could be home within the week. If we can't get to the bottom of this affair by then, brother Mycroft will be returning to his doom...

Music. The stage is reconfigured by the actors playing PARFITT and CHAPPELL, who lurk upstage as:

WATSON	*(To audience)* Holmes and I headed back from Haymarket to Baker Street. The lamps were being lit as we turned onto Woodstock Street, the shadows and fog forming into

147

sinister and unsettling shapes on the cobbles, so how Holmes saw it I'll never know, but at once I heard his voice:

HOLMES   Watson, look out!

HOLMES shoves WATSON to one side. There is a large crash. Music.

WATSON   *(To audience)* Three large bricks shattered to fragments at our feet. *(Exclaiming)* What the devil?

HOLMES   He's not waiting any more.

WATSON   What?

HOLMES   Moriarty. He means to kill us today. We'll take the back streets. Hurry!

HOLMES helps WATSON to his feet. There is a moment of stylised movement, as WATSON says:

WATSON   *(To audience)* Five minutes further on, as we ducked down Seymour Mews...

A figure emerges from the shadows – one of MORIARTY's hired thugs, CHAPPELL.

CHAPPELL   Spare a farthing, guv'nor. Just a farthing.

From another direction a second thug, PARFITT appears.

PARFITT	Not too much to ask, is it?
HOLMES	I'd ask you to stand aside, gentlemen.
CHAPPELL	We're only looking to get us some porter.
PARFITT	P'raps a bit of stew too...
CHAPPELL	Yeah... nice drop of stew...
HOLMES	If you would.
CHAPPELL	Have a heart, squire.
HOLMES	Step behind me, Watson.
PARFITT	Oi. No need to be like that.
HOLMES	On the contrary, Don Chappell, I'd prefer my friend to be as far from that raking cross of yours as possible.

CHAPPELL straightens. The game is up. He's been recognised.

CHAPPELL	Remember me, do you?
HOLMES	Mendoza's Rooms. Last year, wasn't it?
CHAPPELL	Year before. You damn near broke my jaw.
PARFITT	Come on Will. Let's stick 'em and be done.

149

HOLMES   You, sir – I don't believe I've had the pleasure.

PARFITT   Ain't nothing pleasurable about what's going to happen to you two.

Music. PARFITT draws a knife. CHAPPELL does the same.

HOLMES   Final warning. Stand aside.

PARFITT   You must be joking...

There follows a fight; HOLMES taking a couple of licks and WATSON helping a little before HOLMES disarms and gouges CHAPPELL's good eye. PARFITT abandons his attack and picks his friend up from the floor.

This ain't going to stop, you know. Not for you, for him... not for your housekeeper neither. What's left of her.

CHAPPELL   My nose...

WATSON   What do you mean by that?

CHAPPELL   My nose, you bastard.

PARFITT   Watch your backs.

CHAPPELL   Bastard!

CHAPPELL and PARFITT exit.

WATSON   *(Calling after them)* What did you mean by that?

But they're gone.

        (To HOLMES) Are you all right?

HOLMES   Cracked rib possibly. Everything else feels as it should.

WATSON   Mrs. Hudson!

HOLMES   I'll get us a cab!

HOLMES and WATSON exit. The stage is reconfigured. FENNELL enters. He paces, clutching a bowler hat. HOLMES and WATSON enter. FENNELL turns to them. Lights.

FENNELL   Mr. Holmes, sir.

WATSON   Who the Devil are you?

FENNELL   Herbert Fennell.

WATSON   Who?

HOLMES   Archivist at the Times. *(To FENNELL)* Good to see you again. Where's Mrs. Hudson? What's happened to her?

FENNELL   She's all right – just shaken up. I escorted her home.

WATSON   What shook her?

MRS. HUDSON enters, carrying a large book and wincing with every step.

MRS. HUDSON	Long and short of it is, we were all but run down.
HOLMES	By what?
MRS. HUDSON	Two-horse van.

FENNELL helps MRS. HUDSON to the armchair.

WATSON	Dear Lord!
MRS. HUDSON	I'm fine.
FENNELL	You were clipped.
MRS. HUDSON	Could have been worse.

MRS. HUDSON looks at FENNELL with gratitude.

HOLMES	What happened?
FENNELL	Well...
MRS. HUDSON	We'd finished at the archive and Herbert suggested a spot of lunch.
FENNELL	I did.
MRS. HUDSON	Only I wanted to find out a little more about Alma Waters. You know...
HOLMES	The artist who was smothered. Go on.
MRS. HUDSON	So we went to Bedford College where she used to teach, and I... well...

FENNELL	I don't know quite how she managed it –
MRS. HUDSON	Mentioned Mr. Holmes, didn't I? Works a treat most of the time.
WATSON	Managed what?
MRS. HUDSON	To borrow this.

She hands HOLMES the book. He immediately passes it over to WATSON.

	It's a book of Mrs. Waters' sketches. You know, of all her different tenants? In case the police had been onto something.
WATSON	I see.
FENNELL	We came out down Hanover Gate and were crossing onto Park Road –
MRS. HUDSON	There's a tearoom there I happen to like –
FENNELL	And this two-horse van whizzed round and was on us like a flash. Full speed. *(To MRS. HUDSON)* Straight at you, wasn't it?

MRS. HUDSON nods.

MRS. HUDSON	Would have got me, too. Then Herbert grabbed me and saved my life.

FENNELL	It wasn't like that.
MRS. HUDSON	It was! He pulled me up onto the kerb as the van clattered past. Up Park Road and gone. Like it hadn't happened.
HOLMES	*(To FENNELL)* We are in your debt, sir.
FENNELL	Reckon I've been well paid in bun-loaf.
MRS. HUDSON	Never mind bun-loaf. I see cream teas in your future. Help me down these here stairs.
FENNELL	Right-o. We've a celebration to get back to.
WATSON	Celebration?
MRS. HUDSON	Oh, haven't told you, have I? We solved the Rijnders quote.
FENNELL	It were you, not me.
HOLMES	Go on...
MRS. HUDSON	It wasn't exactly what you wanted... peace, and international relations and all that, but it *is* a story from last April.
FENNELL	About a Naval Treaty going missing.

HOLMES and WATSON share a glance.

MRS. HUDSON	Anyway... in case it helps. Come on, you.

MRS. HUDSON and FENNELL exit.

WATSON	It couldn't be.

A beat.

	The Naval treaty? The one that cost dear Percy Phelps his job?
HOLMES	The first phase of his plan. Had I but known.

HOLMES sits and opens Alma Waters' sketchbook. WATSON heads to the window.

WATSON	I won't stand for this, Holmes. How do we take the fight to Moriarty?
HOLMES	We can't. We have nothing over him.
WATSON	The red file?
HOLMES	Useless until we can decode it. I wouldn't stand in the window if I were you.

WATSON moves away from the window.

WATSON	What are we expected to do? Hide in here like a pack of whipped dogs until his plan plays out?
HOLMES	I imagine that's just what he... expects...

A beat. HOLMES comes across something in the book he's looking at.

My word...

He dashes to the table and starts looking at notes and clippings.

You can write me down an ass this time, Watson.

WATSON   Holmes?

HOLMES   This is *not* the fish I expected to catch.

WATSON   We haven't caught anyone yet.

HOLMES snatches up the book and shows it to WATSON.

HOLMES   On the contrary...

WATSON looks at the page. A beat.

Imagine this fellow without the beard.

WATSON   Is that...?

HOLMES   It is.

WATSON   I thought he was dead.

HOLMES   Apparently not.

WATSON   Then he's Alma Waters' killer.

HOLMES   More than just hers.

HOLMES fishes around on the table until he finds the advert that LaROTIÈRE didn't get to put in the papers.

It's time.

WATSON For...?

HOLMES The Scoundrels' Assembly's final performance.

Music. The stage is reconfigured. HOLMES exits.

WATSON *(To audience)* Holmes imposed on Mr. Fennell one more time, asking him to take that last post to *The Times.* The one LaRotière never got to advertise. "Being for the benefit of M. Croft. L'Assemblea dei Furfanti. All tickets sold. Exclusive run opens Sunday. Little Theatre Beneath." The players were ready. The scene set – with nothing less than the future of the Empire at stake...

We have returned to the room below the theatre, LESTRADE and MYCROFT facilitating the change. HOLMES enters carrying the red file. MYCROFT removes his coat and gives it to HOLMES. LESTRADE and MYCROFT exit. HOLMES puts on his brother's coat, sits at the table with his back to the room and begins to read. As the music softens we hear the turning of a key, and into the space steps

DeWILDE. He stands for a moment, looking at the figure at the table. Then he says:

DeWILDE   Mycroft. My God! Where the hell have you been?

HOLMES, dressed as MYCROFT, barely reacts.

You're in a lot of trouble. The people who prepared that file, they... one of them turned on you. I didn't believe it, I have to say, but he presented some fairly compelling evidence. A Black Order was drawn up. By Fitzmaurice. He's had it in for both of us. In fact...

DeWILDE takes a step closer to the table.

...in fact, I think he had that file doctored. Whatever it says, is... is...

HOLMES holds up a silencing finger – he's reading.

It's lies. But we can set it right. I know what to do. The men tasked with carrying out the Black Order... they followed me. Your best course of action, if you wish to get out of this, is to do exactly as I say.

DeWilde approaches the table.

Mycroft.

As DeWILDE draws his sword back in preparation for a thrust, HOLMES turns, revolver drawn.

HOLMES Wrong Holmes, I'm afraid.

DeWILDE takes a step back. Lowers his sword slightly.

Why Sir James, whatever are you doing with that sword in your hand?

DeWILDE I...

HOLMES Please.

DeWILDE puts his sword back in its scabbard. HOLMES refers to the red file.

HOLMES Makes for fascinating reading, this file – once you've mastered the code. Talk you through it, shall I? Perhaps we can pool our resources. Do you mind?

DeWILDE You're the one with the gun.

HOLMES Oh, yes. Sorry.

HOLMES places the gun on the table – though not too far from him.

In essence it tells the story of one man. One ambitious, dangerous man.

DeWILDE Indeed?

HOLMES
Admittedly this man was manipulated by a second, more shadowy figure... alas, there's not a great deal about *him* in here. No, the subject of this red file has had a meteoric rise through the corridors of power until now – thanks to the suspicion thrown upon my brother – he is being readied to take what is currently the most powerful position in world politics. Isn't that right, Sir James?

DeWILDE smiles coldly.

DeWILDE
He said you were bright.

HOLMES
Did he?

DeWILDE
That eventually you'd see at least part of the picture.

HOLMES
Which part? I'm intrigued. Did he assume I'd put together his work behind the scenes, grooming first your covert military career, then clearing the path through government? Exposing scandals, engineering Stock Market collapses to force desperate acts... laying the rungs for your climb to the top. Yes, I suspect he *would* see that, wouldn't he? He might even have suspected that I would figure out who you really

160

are – James Wilder, bastard son of the Duke of Holderness. Who kidnapped his own ten-year-old half-brother from the Priory School all those years ago.

A beat.

Now I recall that to avoid scandal, your father the Duke gave you money and told you to head to Australia. So who put that idea of South Africa in your head, I wonder? Perhaps a teacher... someone you looked up to... at both Stonyhurst College and Durham University? How am I doing so far, Watson?

DeWILDE turns to see WATSON emerging from the shadows. HOLMES hands WATSON the revolver. WATSON points it at DeWILDE.

WATSON   Excellent, I'd say.

HOLMES   You see, you underestimated brother Mycroft. His time away from Whitehall was not spent in hiding from the Black Order. It was spent researching you – the telegram confirming your educational background arriving just this morning. Tell me, James – how long do you think it will take the Professor to realise he's made a mistake, choosing you as his pawn? Considering your limitations.

DeWILDE   What limitations?

WATSON   What Pinel would call *'mania sans délire.'*

HOLMES   To use a modern idiom, you're a psychopath.

DeWILDE turns from WATSON to HOLMES.

How else to describe it? You assassinated your former comrades. Stabbed LaRotière in the neck with my brother's letter opener. Beat Kurzenov to death in Madrid. Plunged a knife through Eduardo Lucas' heart. Killed and dismembered Adolphus Meyer – mere days before our first meeting, in fact.

DeWILDE   Impressive.

HOLMES   You might have gotten away with all of those crimes too... had it not been for the one murder we've not mentioned. Alma Waters.

WATSON   "The innocent seldom find an uneasy pillow."

HOLMES   I suspected you were James Wilder from your reactions to Derbyshire, where you grew up... it's why I asked Mycroft to take time away from his work and look into you – but it wasn't until I saw the late Mrs. Waters' sketch book that I realised why she, and all the other Scoundrels, had to die. And why you left Miss Adler until last.

DeWILDE   Why's that?

WATSON   Heterochromia.

DeWILDE turns back to WATSON.

I'm no artist, but Alma Waters' picture brought out the contrast very well. Sketching eyes of two different colours must be hard. Almost as hard as hiding the condition.

HOLMES has approached DeWILDE from behind.

HOLMES   When we saw Miss Waters' wonderful drawing of her tenant, we knew that at some point between returning from South Africa and then reinventing yourself as the politician Sir James deWilde...

Gently, HOLMES removes the eyepatch.

You were Jan Rijnders. Dutch spy, and founder of the Scoundrels' Assembly. The report of your torture and death in Persia was a fake. You posted the first quote to your former friends yourself. And then spent the next two years planning their murders – couldn't risk them exposing you, after all. And now it's over.

That's enough for DeWILDE. With bewildering speed he hits HOLMES in the stomach, swinging around WATSON and disarming him in one fluid move. He then aims the pistol at HOLMES and pulls the trigger. There is a click – the gun is empty. He tosses it to WATSON and draws his sword.

DeWILDE   Well played Mr. Holmes. You're more than I expected, I'll admit.

HOLMES groans in acknowledgment.

WATSON   Holmes?

HOLMES   I'm all right.

WATSON   Know how you'll explain our disappearance, do you?

DeWILDE   Your fates will be shared with everyone else at the theatre tonight. You'll burn.

DeWILDE draws an envelope from his pocket.

And once the theatre's destroyed and you two are gone, the letter I killed Lucas for – *this* letter – will be sent. Wars will start, wars that can't be stopped, and the Prime Minister will realise he needs a new Mycroft. Someone with an eye for strategy. And who else but your brother's favourite student? I'll be signed into position, and I'll. Run. Everything. The pen truly is mightier than the sword, you see? Though the sword will make me richer. Much, much richer.

HOLMES   Blood money, every penny.

DeWILDE   You count the blood. I'll count the money.

WATSON   How could you? You were knighted! Have you no honour?

DeWILDE   I have honour enough.

WATSON   You'll be caught. Brought to account.

DeWILDE   By you? You'll be dead. Who else is left?

ADLER enters as she did the first time we saw her.

ADLER   You know, for someone who spent their whole life in intelligence...

DeWILDE   Irene.

ADLER   Not another word.

165

She stares at him. Draws her sword.

> They were our friends. Our brothers!

They begin to circle one another.

DeWILDE For what it's worth...

ADLER Nothing. It's worth nothing. Now drop that sword or go to work.

A swordfight, at the end of which ADLER has defeated DeWILDE.

DeWILDE Irene. Irene, listen, listen, listen... come with me. Think about it. Think about it. We can do this together. Kill these two and the world is ours. No-one else needs know. No-one else *will* know.

ADLER Oh, Jan...

HOLMES *(Calling off)* Gentlemen.

LESTRADE and MYCROFT enter. DeWILDE looks shocked.

WATSON Did you forget the door to the theatre?

ADLER All yours Inspector.

LESTRADE James Wilder, I am arresting you for crimes of high treason, and for the murders of Yevgeny Kurzenov,

Adolphus Meyer, Louis LaRotière, Eduardo Lucas and Alma Waters.

DeWILDE A public trial will be painful. Not just to me but to the government as a whole.

MYCROFT Perhaps. But not half as painful as that long drop to the end of the rope.

LESTRADE moves towards the exit with DeWILDE.

DeWILDE *(To ADLER)* I really did love you, you know.

ADLER You've been spending too much time with politicians.

LESTRADE exits with DeWILDE.

MYCROFT Well, Sherlock, as charming as Bohemia was, do remind me never to get tangled up in one of these affairs again.

WATSON *(To HOLMES)* He was in *Bohemia?*

HOLMES I told you his Majesty owed me a favour.

MYCROFT *(To HOLMES)* You were right about his library. First rate.

He looks at his watch.

Time to get back to the club. There's a silent booth with my name on it...

MYCROFT exits. HOLMES takes the key from around his neck.

HOLMES   This belongs to you.

ADLER   You cracked LaRotière's code then?

HOLMES   That? Good Lord no.

ADLER   But – everything you said... the way he responded...

HOLMES   One can do wonders with the balance of probability.

ADLER   *(To WATSON)* He really was the smart one after all, huh?

ADLER kisses HOLMES on the cheek again.

Take care of yourself, Sherlock.

She exits. HOLMES sits carefully, holding his ribs.

WATSON   I thought we were done for that time.

HOLMES   Not yet.

WATSON   Not yet? It's over, isn't it?

HOLMES   Not by a long chalk. I fear we've rather upset the hornets' nest. The Professor will not take the news of his acolyte's capture well; we must draw his sting far from those we care

168

about. Your dear Mary, our Mrs. Hudson...

WATSON   How do we do that?

HOLMES   By giving his ire a focus.

A beat.

I wonder, my dear Watson, if you'd be willing to accompany me on a trip.

WATSON   Where to?

HOLMES   The continent.

Music. The stage is reconfigured, people moving furniture, carrying bags, blowing whistles &c. A physical sequence. HOLMES and WATSON sit together; there is the sound of a steam train powering through the countryside.

WATSON   *(To audience)* From Victoria the following morning we travelled to the coast and crossed the Channel in surprisingly clear weather.

The pair stand, move across the stage, the other actors bringing cases, chairs &c. across to a different position, creating, briefly, the image of the pair of them on board a ship. They wave, we hear the sounds of the sea... and we move on again.

At Dieppe we headed for Strasbourg, then crossed the border into Switzerland.

Once more the seats, luggage &c. are shifted, with HOLMES & WATSON sitting together. The music may take in a slightly different flavour (or perhaps the instrumentation alters) as the characters pass through different countries.

Reaching Geneva we made our way over the Gemmi Pass, still deep in snow, and pushed on to Meiringen by way of Interlaken.

Another train whistle. Another sequence.

There had been no sign of Moriarty, and though Holmes was ever watchful, his spirits were higher than I had seen them in weeks. Had I but known we were approaching our final destination...

WATSON sits back. Music fades, replaced by the insistent rattle of a train. HOLMES is now looking at the horizon through binoculars.

HOLMES Let's stop at Meiringen a while. There's a hotel there that should suit us quite well – the Englischer Hof. And it's close to the Falls at Reichenbach – spectacular by all accounts; we should see them up close.

A beat.

Grim news from Lestrade, I take it.

WATSON	I beg your pardon?
HOLMES	The telegram in your pocket. It's from the Inspector.

WATSON removes it.

WATSON	It is... but...

HOLMES lowers the binoculars.

HOLMES	You've mentioned your beloved Mary at least three times daily until the day before last – Mrs. Hudson too, I might add. Clearly you wished to find out if they were free of the Professor's wrath, but contacting them directly would be too worrisome, so who else could you trust? You sent Lestrade a message on Tuesday which relaxed you somewhat until this morning, when your countenance darkened. Not enough to indicate harm, yet there's dirty work afoot.

A beat.

So?

WATSON hands HOLMES the telegram. Lights up on LESTRADE in a special. Music under:

LESTRADE	Mary & Mrs. Hudson both fine. Glad to hear you're safe. Saw what had happened to Baker Street and

feared the worst. Fire gutted top two floors. No casualties. Travel safe. L.

LESTRADE exits. Music fades. HOLMES and WATSON look out in silence for a moment. The sound of burning can be heard low in the mix.

WATSON   I didn't know how to bring it up.

HOLMES   Because...?

WATSON   It's your home! He destroyed your home!

HOLMES   Tried to, at least.

WATSON   We need to go back.

HOLMES looks at WATSON.

                    You were wrong. He hasn't followed us at all.

HOLMES   Most certainly he has. And he has every malevolent eye in Europe trained on looking for us. You think he himself burned Baker Street? No, this is his endgame. He will remain in our blind spot; his lackeys baiting us to expose ourselves until he is ready to strike.

WATSON   How can you be sure?

HOLMES   It's what I'd do.

A beat. The sounds of fire fade out.

172

He has nothing left. There is to be no second war; his pawn is for the gallows and his poison can spread no further. All that remains is the desire to revenge himself upon me personally.

WATSON   Maybe he'll never get the chance.

HOLMES   How's that?

WATSON   You've made a good living as a consulting detective. If you were to stop it all now, remain on the continent... you could still say that London had been the sweeter for your presence. Walk away. Return to your scientific experiments.

HOLMES   But I could not rest, Watson, I could not sit easy in my chair knowing that he was out there somewhere. I swear, your memoirs will draw to an end the day I crown my career with his capture. Or his extinction.

WATSON takes out a flask and raises it.

WATSON   To Baker Street.

HOLMES nods.

If, on our return, you're in need of a room, Mary and I...

HOLMES smiles. Cleans the lenses of his binoculars.

	I'll miss the place.
HOLMES	Of course you will.
WATSON	Is that to say that you won't?
HOLMES	No, I recognise the comfort of the familiar as much as anyone.

HOLMES looks at WATSON.

	Do you believe me incapable of feeling?
WATSON	Not at all.
HOLMES	The descriptions of me, in your accounts... that's not just dramatic licence, is it?
WATSON	You said you hadn't read the stories.
HOLMES	I didn't say that.
WATSON	Oh....?
HOLMES	No. I said I hadn't enjoyed them.
WATSON	Ah.

HOLMES gives WATSON a look. WATSON smiles.

HOLMES	It's the resources as much as anything.
WATSON	Resources?

HOLMES	At Baker Street. Scientific papers, histories... all that knowledge, now just... so much ash.
WATSON	Well... with a mind like yours nothing's truly lost.

HOLMES smiles sadly.

HOLMES	Except time.

Music. They shift positions.

WATSON	*(To audience)* We reached the Englischer Hof and stayed for two days. On the third, Holmes and I headed out to the falls.
HOLMES	Watson! This way!
WATSON	*(To audience)* It is a fearful place. A full hour's hike on foam worn rocks leads to a crescent-shaped path, cut around the falls. The torrent, swollen by melting snow, plunges into a tremendous abyss, from which the spray rolls up like smoke from a burning house.
HOLMES	It's magnificent!
WATSON	*(To audience)* Holmes stood near the edge, peering down at the gleam of the breaking water far below us against the black rocks, near

deafened by the incessant roar. With no little difficulty, I joined him.

Throughout his narration WATSON has been edging towards HOLMES so that at its end they are standing together.

HOLMES   Power.

WATSON   What's that?

HOLMES   Again and again over the years, we have seen those – through weakness, through greed – seek to steal their fleeting moments of power. And then you look at this, and it's all so...

He lets the sentence trail. A MESSENGER enters.

MESSENGER   Doctor? Doctor Watson?

WATSON turns and sees him.

WATSON   Hello, yes?

MESSENGER   I've been sent by the hotelier. There's an English woman, sick with consumption. She has been overtaken with a haemorrhage.

WATSON   A haemorrhage, you say?

MESSENGER   She would receive great comfort from seeing an English physician.

WATSON looks at HOLMES.

HOLMES   Go.

WATSON   If you're sure...

HOLMES   Yes. Go back. I intend to climb to
                   the highest part of the falls. You
                   couldn't follow me anyway. I'll
                   return later and we'll supper
                   together.

*Music. WATSON makes his way over to the
MESSENGER, who beckons him follow and then
exits. HOLMES takes out his binoculars once more.*

WATSON   *(To audience)* As I left Holmes, he
                   was staring out at the snow-flecked
                   pines across the valley from the falls.
                   Visual displays of joy were infrequent
                   with him... but I must say he looked
                   content.

*With a last look back, WATSON exits. A beat, then
MORIARTY enters. Without looking round,
HOLMES says:*

HOLMES   One of yours, I assume. The
                   messenger.

MORIARTY smiles. He nods.

                   And I thought you were keen on
                   meeting the doctor.

MORIARTY   We're past that now, wouldn't you
                   agree?

*MORIARTY steps closer to HOLMES. They look at
the falls for a moment.*

Spectacular.

HOLMES There's a higher viewpoint.

MORIARTY There is.

HOLMES takes a notepad and pencil from his satchel.

HOLMES Would you permit me...?

MORIARTY looks at him.

He's bound to return. I'd like to leave a few words.

MORIARTY *(Thinking aloud)* An hour back to the hotel...

HOLMES An hour and ten, with Watson's leg.

MORIARTY The journey back...

He thinks it over.

By all means.

HOLMES Thank you.

MORIARTY I'm not entirely monstrous. That's my curse.

HOLMES begins to write. A beat.

I wish you'd done as I asked. Backed away.

HOLMES An impossibility.

MORIARTY	That's *your* curse.
HOLMES	Why did you do it?
MORIARTY	Which part?
HOLMES	Any of it.
MORIARTY	The thrust and parry of our previous entanglements, as fun as they have been, played out within a largely inflexible legal structure. I sought a way to change the rules of engagement. Control the truth, and what is 'good;' what is 'right...' they become far more malleable concepts.
HOLMES	'Good' and 'right' never change.
MORIARTY	Of course they do. Once you dam up the flow of truth, you can hold back words like 'good' and 'right' until they're useful.
HOLMES	You would wilfully push the world so close to corruption?
MORIARTY	Push it? It's already there.

HOLMES does not reply. He continues to write.

> The inequity. The anger. And the masses, desperate for a voice, desperate for change... none of them realising that those "voices" can be

	shaped; the "change" controlled. Driven. Towards... well. Anything.
HOLMES	War?
MORIARTY	A market's a market.
HOLMES	Not everyone can be bought and sold.
MORIARTY	Every man has their price. From the poorhouse to the politicians.
HOLMES	I'm afraid you're wrong.
MORIARTY	You're afraid I'm not.

MORIARTY laughs suddenly. It is laughter more commonly shared between friends.

Have you never imagined it? Your intellect, my vision? Together?

HOLMES — My imagination begins and ends with freeing society of your chaos.

MORIARTY simply shakes his head, a smile on his face. His note now finished, HOLMES puts the notepad back in his satchel. Looks around.

Here, I think.

He places the satchel close to one of the entrances, then turns back to MORIARTY.

MORIARTY — Come, then. It's late.

HOLMES — As you wish...

Music. There then follows a desperate combat, fought between adversaries who speak between feints, parries, blows and counterblows.

MORIARTY   You've been a worthy adversary. I'm aware of my own capabilities of course, but you...

Another thrust, another parry.

Tell me you don't feel the same.

HOLMES   Your faith in your own intellect is one thing, but using it to justify the manipulation of democracy?

MORIARTY   Politics is too important to be left to the politicians. It requires a much defter hand.

HOLMES   Yours?

MORIARTY   Why not?

HOLMES   That's tyranny.

MORIARTY   It's order.

MORIARTY climbs to the top of the viewing platform (our stairs).

The masses you've spent your whole career serving – the ones that clean the streets, serve at tables, fight in wars; they don't fight for governments. Flags. Borders. And they certainly don't fight for democracy. They fight for me. And global 'tyrants' just like me. Whisperers in ears, power brokers... we have many names. What you call tyranny I call an opportunity. You got in the way of that this time, but you're no barrier. You're a bump in the road. Nothing more.

HOLMES has joined MORIARTY at the top of the platform.

HOLMES Unless there is no road.

MORIARTY Unless there is no road.

They both look over the edge. MORIARTY extends a hand.

Join me.

HOLMES looks at him.

Come on! We'd be unstoppable!

A beat.

Join me.

HOLMES *(Smiling)* Gladly.

And suddenly we're into slow-motion, HOLMES wrapping his arms around MORIARTY and attempting to propel the pair of them over the edge of the falls. As this happens, the lights strobe slowly, giving us snapshot images of this final moment. The music comes up and we hear HOLMES' voice, reading out the note he left for WATSON to find:

HOLMES

(Rec'd) Dear Watson. I write these few lines through the courtesy of Professor Moriarty, who awaits our final discussion even now. I am pleased to think that I shall be able to free society from any further effects of his presence, though I fear that it is at a cost which will give pain to my friends, and especially, my dear Watson, to you.

A huge boom and swell in both waterfall and music as the combatants lean seemingly over the railings. A final roar from both of them and we snap to black and hold for a moment. HOLMES and MORIARTY exit. The sound of the waterfall slowly fades and music underscores the continuation of the letter as the lights lift on the now all but empty shell of Baker Street, WATSON and MRS. HUDSON standing as at the beginning, MRS. HUDSON reading the letter. Her voice mingles with HOLMES', and eventually takes over as his fades out.

I can only apologise for the upset caused, for I always knew it to be unavoidable. And so I go to cut off the head of the snake. Pray give my greetings to Mrs. Watson, say goodbye to...

MRS. HUDSON (*With HOLMES initially*) Pray give my greetings to Mrs. Watson, say goodbye to dear Mrs. Hudson, and believe me to be, my dear fellow, very sincerely yours. Sherlock Holmes.

Lights.

Well. That's it then.

She hands the letter back to WATSON. A beat.

There's no way he might... *(have survived the fall)*

WATSON shakes his head.

No. No.

Looking at the devastation around him, WATSON moves downstage as if to a window.

It's not as bad as they're saying. Bit of brickwork, lick of paint...

WATSON gives a slight shrug.

I was out at the theatre when it went up. I've been staying with... you know...

A beat.

Funny. All the cases, and... comes to this.

WATSON	Will you come back? If it can be put right.
MRS. HUDSON	Here?
WATSON	It's your home.
MRS. HUDSON	I mean, I *would*. If I thought he... if I thought...

A beat.

You know.

WATSON	Of course.

A FIREMAN enters. He is played by the same actor playing HOLMES. He is carrying a box of scorched possessions.

FIREMAN	I'm going to have to ask you to vacate, sir. Ma'am.
WATSON	One more minute? Please.
FIREMAN	No longer.

The FIREMAN watches for a moment, then exits.

MRS. HUDSON	It's a mercy he didn't get to see it this way.
WATSON	It is.

A beat.

He really was the best... and the wisest man I have ever known.

A beat.

              Come on, Mrs. Aspinall.

MRS. HUDSON   Don't. You'll set me off again.

WATSON and MRS. HUDSON stare out of the window... Then we hear the first strains of a violin motif, as if played from just outside the door. MRS HUDSON and WATSON turn together as the lights fade to black.

The End.